Rebel Spirits

Also by Lois Ruby

THE SECRET OF LAUREL OAKS

Rebel
Spirits

BY LOIS RUBY

Point

Library of Congress Cataloging-in-Publication Data

Ruby, Lois.

Rebel spirits / by Lois Ruby. — 1st ed.

p. cm.

Summary: Sixteen-year-old Lorelei is not happy when her family moves into an old
bed-and-breakfast in Gettysburg, Pennsylvania — and that is before she meets the
Civil War ghost, Nathaniel, who needs her help, and discovers that some of the hotel
staff are not what they seem to be.

ISBN 978-0-545-42623-7

1. Bed and breakfast accommodations — Juvenile fiction. 2. Haunted hotels —
Juvenile fiction. 3. Gettysburg (Pa.) — Juvenile fiction. 4. Ghost stories. [1. Bed and
breakfast accommodations — Fiction. 2. Haunted places — Fiction. 3. Ghosts —
Fiction. 4. Gettysburg (Pa.) — Fiction. 5. Mystery and detective stories.] I. Title.

PZ7.R8314Reb 2013

813.54 — dc23

2012035277

12 11 10 9 8 7 6 5 4 3 2 1   13 14 15 16 17/0

Printed in the U.S.A.   23

First edition, June 2013

For the real *Jocelyn Charlotte, Hannah Miriam,*
Jacob Chase, Jacob Maxwell, Evan Charles,
and especially for Abigail Fay

Water, gentlemen, is the one substance
from which the earth can conceal nothing. It sucks out its
innermost secrets and brings them to our very lips.

JEAN GIRAUDOUX,
The Madwoman of Chaillot

I asked these spirit figures if I was seeing them
or if I was seeing what was in my own brain.
They answered, "both."

EILEEN GARRETT
(A Twentieth-Century Medium)

1

I CANNOT BELIEVE we're moving into that creaky old bed-and-breakfast," I mutter for about the hundredth time. The Taurus is stop-starting in morning rush-hour traffic heading toward I-76. We're leaving *home* in Philadelphia, driving to *not-home* in Gettysburg. My parents have this insane whim that we need a real picket-fenced house in small-town America.

My dog, Gertie, and I are sandwiched between U-Haul boxes and Mom's Tiffany lamp that's mummified in bubble wrap. Gertie's got her paws on the window longingly. She doesn't want to leave Philly any more than I do. I speak for us both: "You bought the place without my vote."

"Lorelei Cordelia, be rational."

I open my mouth in rebuttal, but Dad's quick.

"You're sixteen years old."

"Nearly seventeen," I snap.

He catches my eye in the rearview. "Your input is always valuable, but your mother and I make the final decisions."

I sigh. So, what good has it done me living in Philadelphia, the home of the cracked Liberty Bell, when I have no liberty? My big brother, Randy, escaped this disastrous move by going to Ghana with the Peace Corps. Easy way out.

"Honey, it'll be so nice at the Coolspring Inn; you'll see," Mom says.

Nice pops up in every third sentence because Mom herself is so . . . nice.

"Small town," she goes on, "lovely salt-of-the-earth people, a beautiful old house with rich history. Our bed-and-breakfast will be filled with fascinating guests from around the world."

"Tourists."

"Guests in our home, Lori," Mom reaffirms.

"With the nineteenth-century plumbing. Is there even an indoor toilet?"

"Several. It's got fully reconditioned plumbing," Dad says merrily. "No outhouse."

Mom croons, "And you'll have such a nice, memorable school year."

Senior year as a total stranger. How could they do this to me?

"You didn't like it when we moved from that Harrisburg hotel to Philly," Mom reminds me, "and look how well it turned out."

Mom and Dad met in college as hospitality industry majors, so Randy and I are hotel rats, living in one hotel after another. Until six o'clock this morning, my home was the New Century Plaza in downtown Philadelphia. There was a fitness center, a rooftop pool, and a presidential suite — never actually used by *the* president. Our apartment was on the sixteenth floor. My best friend, Jocelyn, and I practically lived on Cheetos and peanut-butter crackers that we got for free out of the vending machines.

"That's awful," Jocelyn had moaned last month when I'd told her about the great injustice my parents were doing me. "Gettysburg is totally the anti-Philadelphia. You'll wilt like lettuce out there in the boonies, Lori. Besides," she'd added, sniffling back tears, "how can you leave the love of your life?" A joke, since I'm sort of crazy about Danny Bartoli, but he thinks of me as furniture — comfortable, but not the kind you'd want to have in your room. Oh, well, he's a Napoleonic five foot five, and I'm at least three gigantic inches taller. I'd end up a hunchback from stooping to dance with him.

"I'll leave Danny to you in my will," I told Jos, laughing through my own tears. But to myself, I said, *I'll die if he hits on her.*

Jocelyn has been my best friend since the seventh grade. We first bonded over our shared interest in the sisters Margaret and Kate Fox. Way back in 1847, they were not much older than us, and already famous for holding séances in their front parlor. Meaning they talked to the dead, who answered back.

So what if they were total frauds? We didn't care. We wanted to be just like them. We wanted to *be* them: outrageously rebellious free spirits. They were my consolation as I began towering over the gnome-sized boys in sixth and seventh grade.

So, Jos and I found a Ouija board at a garage sale, and we ordered a genuine fake crystal ball online. We hung black sheets over the windows in her basement and put ghoulish-green lightbulbs in the lamps, and perfected corny voices somewhere between Yoda and the *Sesame Street* Count. We charged everyone fifty cents for a glimpse into their future, a dollar if they wanted to hear actual knocks and squeals from the dead. We told them the names of boyfriends who'd adore them in high school and how gorgeous (not to mention rich) they'd be after their braces came off and they got modeling jobs. Guys, too. Everybody knew it was a game, and it financed trips to the mall and iTunes purchases for Jos and me. It was way more fun than babysitting.

But then one day I saw something in the crystal ball — a child falling out of a tree. He was twisted and motionless on the hard ground, with his glasses unbroken next to him. I knew he was dead. Jos didn't see a thing. How could that be? It was as clear as day. The next morning I read the headline on my laptop:

DELAWARE COUNTY SEVEN-YEAR-OLD
PLUNGES TO HIS DEATH

I couldn't watch the video. I'd already seen enough.

That was ninth grade, the last time we did a séance, but not the last time I peered into some other universe that wasn't plain old reality. I never told anyone about the other times, not even Jos, and I forced myself to forget them. In fact, I made a big point of being skeptical about unexplainable things.

Now, inching through traffic on our way to Gettysburg, Mom speaks up again, and I'm pulled out of thoughts of ghosts and the dead.

"I'm sure Gertie will love being a country dog," Mom is saying, "where she can roam free."

Gertie looks up at me with those sweet blue-ringed Australian shepherd eyes. She takes my side in every family dispute, so she's dead set against Gettysburg. Earlier this morning I twisted my impossibly straight brown hair into a knot, shaded my hazel eyes with aviator glasses, and took Gertie on a nostalgic strut through Rittenhouse Square. She sniffed every inch of the ground, like she knew it was her last romp through this park. Now she snorts, which says it all.

Dad clutches the steering wheel like it's threatening to escape. "Lorelei, you know about Abraham Lincoln's famous 'four score and seven years ago' address that he delivered at Gettysburg, don't you?"

"Yes, Dad. We had to memorize it in eighth grade." Who knew that four years later I'd end up with a Gettysburg address of my own?

"Good, well, here's a crash course in local history."

"Honey, don't say *crash* while we're driving," Mom cuts in.

"Slip of the tongue, Miriam, sorry," my dad says. He smiles at me in the rearview mirror and I can't help but smile back, even as I steel myself for his history lesson.

"Plant yourself back in 1863," my dad begins. "The middle of the Civil War. Nobody expects the Confederates to head so far north, but sure enough General Lee leads the Confederate army right into the line of fire in Gettysburg, Pennsylvania. There's a bloody battle between North and South over the course of three days: July first, second, and third. By the end, thousands are dead and wounded, but the Rebs — that is, the Confederate army — are forced out in defeat, and the Union stands tall."

"How *many* thousands dead and wounded?" I ask, shivering.

"Something close to fifty thousand," Dad replies, braking slowly while the car ahead of us flashes a turn signal. "The whole town of eight thousand citizens was thrown into a tizzy. It's still recovering from those three days and those lost souls. They reenact the entire battle a couple times a year: uniforms, guns, horses, the whole spectacle, I hear."

I wonder about this, stroking Gertie's back. If it was such a horrible battle, why would they want to keep reliving it? "But it's been about a hundred and fifty years," I say, calculating. "Isn't it time they got over it?"

Mom pats Dad's shoulder and turns around to me, practically bumping into Gertie's nose. "Honey, be nice. You know we've been eager to get out of the corporate-hotel rat race. This has always been our family's dream, to run our own cozy little inn in a small town with rich history."

"Humph," I mutter into Gertie's fur. My dream is to win a beach volleyball game, and then take a dip in the ocean. Icy raspberry lemonade will be delivered to me by a surfer boy with golden hair. My dream is definitely not moldering in Gettysburg, Pennsylvania, population: eight thousand people obsessed with a bloody past.

I doze a bunch of miles and wake to the *putt-putt* of a lawn-mower. I open my eyes and register that the huge expanse of blindingly green lawn sloping down to the road is ours. Coolspring Inn. Gertie's wrangling her way around the Tiffany lamp to get a closer look out the window.

Dad slows, as if he's approaching a sacred shrine. A cold sweat sweeps over me. No turning back now.

The shirtless guy riding on the mower checks us out as we pull into the gravel driveway. He is maybe a year older than me, and as tan as a muffin, with longish blond hair sweaty on his shoulders. He reminds me of a border collie.

"Welcome to Coolspring Inn." He flashes a grin, overflowing with cheer. "Evan Maxwell, at your service." He tips an imaginary hat, and his grin widens to an orthodontist's dream job. "You're the Chases, right?" He ducks his head to get a closer look. At me? No, at Gertie, who's halfway out the window. "I'll be done here in a minute." More teeth.

I glance up at the house looming ahead — three gloomy gothic stories, and an attic with oval, stained-glass windows and two turrets. At the top is a circular room with a roof that looks like a blue slate dunce cap. Definitely spooky.

"Welcome to your new home," Evan says.

I study the round room at the top of the house. A shadow passes in one of the windows. Is someone up there, or is it just a trick of the sunlight?

"Let's go in, Vernon. I'm anxious to see if everything looks the way I remember." Mom swings her door open, and Gertie leaps over the front seat to be the first out.

The wraparound porch has a bunch of rocking chairs and a two-seater swing with faded, striped seats. Gertie sniffs under them for evidence of a friend, then squats and marks her territory.

"Gertie!" Mom scolds, and Gertie looks apologetic as her shame leaks through a gap in the floor slats.

The front door is fire-engine red. Curious. Everything else is carved gray stone and blue trim, so why would they paint this door red? The only other hint of color is a small red flag the size of a handkerchief hanging over the front door like mistletoe. To the right of the door is a small brass plate, encrusted with age. I can barely make out the words:

VIENNA CARMODY HOUSE

EST. 1878

"Isn't it marvelous?" Mom gushes, giving the pineapple-shaped knocker two taps.

"No need to knock, Miriam, it's all ours, lock, stock, and barrel." Dad pulls a ring of keys out of his pocket. The fourth one does it. He throws back the door so we get the full effect of Coolspring Inn: gloomy and silent as a tomb. I take in the faded velvet and brocade furniture, the peeling wallpaper, and the threadbare carpeting on the dark stairs that stretch as far as I can see, up to that round room. The air is cloying and thick and smells musty, like a wet winter coat. My heart drops to my ankles. I can't wake up every morning in a dreary house like this. No wonder the previous owners sold it!

Gertie scuttles up the stairs and peers down at us, as if to say, *Whatchu waitin' for, cowards?*

"Careful, Gertie," Mom warns. "The bannister's a little unstable, but the house has good bones, right, Lori?"

"Maybe decaying under the basement," I agree, snickering. Dad had told me that the house was built over a battlefield hospital, once strewn with bodies. Dead bodies seem to be a feature that boosts the value of everything in Gettysburg.

"Not that kind of bones, honey. I mean the frame, the structure. It just needs a little cosmetic work."

Dad gazes around and says, "We'll need to fix up the carpeting and fortify the banister, add a couple coats of paint for the scuffed wainscoting, repair a few boards in the floor, get a few dozen new lightbulbs, and we'll be shipshape."

"The freezer's on the blink, too, don't ya know."

We all jump as a woman materializes from a back room.

"Oh, hello." Mom clutches her throat. "You startled me."

"This house'll do that to a body. Name's Bertha Dryden, and I know who you are: the Chases from Philadelphia," she says with a sneer. A frenzied bunch of hair wound into a bun sits at the top of her pie-shaped head, above big brown eyes with nearly invisible eyelashes. She's wearing a green cotton dress dotted with stemmed cherries. The awful thing is tied at the waist, cutting her into two round sausages.

"The realtor didn't tell us about you," Mom says, "but it's lovely to meet you."

"You are . . . ?" asks Dad.

"Didn't I just say? Bertha Dryden. That realtor woman musta told you the house comes with a staff."

"Something about that," Dad says vaguely. "We haven't made any staffing decisions yet."

"None to make. Here before you stands the executive house manager. I'll tell you up front, I don't vacuum or wash floors. Windows, *pfft*, forget it. We've got a girl from the college, name's Charlotte, who does the heavy lifting, cleans the commodes and all. I supervise."

She sure sounds like she does.

"Yes, well . . ." Dad begins.

"See out there?" Bertha Dryden's wave directs us to a parlor window.

I think maybe I'll get another look at Evan Maxwell, but instead there's a man stooped over a wild profusion of summer flowers. He definitely needs to hitch up the back of his pants. "That's Old Dryden, my other half. Not the better half, mind you. Then there's that Maxwell boy who does whatnot on the house computers and calls himself a landscape artist. Ha! The rest of the staff's Hannah Boedeker, the half-baked cook. She only comes when she's called." Bertha's voice echoes through the empty hall.

"Thank you, Mrs. Dryden," Dad says with a frown. "We'll maintain the status quo until we see what help we need. Mrs. Chase and Lorelei and I expect to do most of the work ourselves."

We do?

"Wouldn't advise it," Bertha replies. "House and grounds

like this takes a whole lot of back-bending care. Well, now, who's this cute mutt?"

Gertie slinks away from Bertha's touch. My dog doesn't appreciate being called a mutt.

I detect slight horror in Mom's voice as she speaks. "You don't live in the house, do you, Bertha?"

"Not on your life! You couldn't pay me enough to stay here past midnight. Bewitching hour, right, mutt?" Bertha raises her pink ballet slipper to scratch Gertie's underbelly. That's Gertie's secret passion, and now Bertha's her new best friend.

"Don't suppose that realtor woman told you. Well, no, she wouldn't, not if she wanted to collect a pretty commission, and don't think I'm not privy to what you paid for this place."

My ears perk up. "Told us what?"

"About the house. It's haunted."

"Oh, I doubt that," Mom says with a nervous laugh, and Bertha tosses her a disapproving glare.

A chill goes through me. I do feel *something* here, as though unseen eyes are watching us. "Is that woman you mentioned, Hannah, in the house?"

"Lord-a-mercy, no. We just use her for breakfasts when there's guests in the house and for scheduled events." Bertha says *events* as though they're as joyful as public hangings. "Well," she adds, "I've got a load working in the laundry room.

Give me a holler if you need anything." With that, she pirou-
ettes on her pink slippers and plods to the darkened back rooms.

Mom and Dad turn to each other and start to whisper,
probably about Bertha and other logistics of the inn. Meanwhile,
I walk to the foot of the stairs and gaze up, ready to inspect that
round room at the top of the house. I'm going to claim it as my
bedroom. Mom and Dad owe me that much for uprooting me
and dragging me across Pennsylvania to this creepy mansion
in the middle of Nowhere, USA.

Which, it turns out, might be haunted.

2

RANDY? I HEAR you, but there's no video."

My brother's postage-stamp-sized face is on my Skype screen, frozen four thousand miles away. There's a three-second voice delay getting the message between here and Ghana.

"Let me poke a few keys," he says. "Reception's spotty. Anything moving?"

"Not yet."

While waiting for my brother to appear, I gaze around at my new surroundings. Up here in the little round bedroom — Mom and Dad agreed to my request — it's hot enough to steam artichokes. It took a zillion trips up the stairs to get all my stuff in here, and now cartons are stacked to the ceiling, and a pile of clothes crests on my bed, which is an island in the middle of the room. Where do you put a bed when all the walls are round? And the bed frame is so tall you have to climb on a stepstool. You can't just flop down on it unless you drop from the ceiling like a gecko. There's no closet — just a narrow wardrobe cabinet that holds about six hangers. Back in Gettysburg times, did people just wear the same muslin frock until it disintegrated?

"Got you on screen. See me yet?" Randy asks.

I turn to see the screen light up. "There you are." The sight of my brother's familiar dark hair and hazel eyes coaxes a smile out of my grumpy self. "Hey, Randy, where are all the students who usually swarm around you?"

"Asleep. It's three a.m. here."

"Oops."

"That's okay," he assures me with a gaping yawn. "What's up?"

"My room. It's like Rapunzel's tower at the top of this creepy house that smells like the inside of your bowling bag. I better keep growing my hair in case I need to escape."

Randy flashes me a sleepy smile. "Sounds pretty cool."

"Also hot, but it's not that bad. Problem is, there's no bath-room up here. I've got to run down a flight of rickety stairs. Hey, who's that behind you?"

Randy looks over his shoulder. "Nobody. Like I said, it's three in the morning."

"No, see him? Wait, he's not in your picture. He's behind *me*!" I spin around, my heart racing, but there's nobody there. "Guess I'm just spooked by this monstrous old house."

I look back at the screen, at my brother's murky-jerky image, and then at mine down in the left-hand corner. And then I see him again. Not Randy. A guy hovering behind me, only partly in camera range.

For a moment I think of the shadowy figure I saw in the window up here when we arrived. Light tricks.

But then the image is clear and true for a second.

"Someone's here!" I hiss.

He's tall, dressed in a rumpled soldier's uniform. His face, shadowed with dark stubble, stares back at me, his deep-set eyes a luminous black. There is such pain in those eyes; they tug at my heart. In that split second of clarity, he's not at all threatening. He's reaching out to me.

The image begins to swim, shimmery and elusive. And then it's gone, and the sympathy I felt cools to fear, freezes to terror. *Someone was in my room!* My teeth start chattering. Has the temperature suddenly dropped forty degrees? I'm tuning in to Randy's words, which were only background noise for a few seconds.

"I don't see anything." Randy's voice is tight with alarm. "Move the laptop around so the camera can pick up what you see."

I jump up, jerking the laptop toward where I saw the figure. The video image shows a canyon of packing boxes, a deer-antler coatrack, empty shelves, the dim bulbs of the chandelier. Not a soul anywhere.

Randy's disembodied computer voice blares out. "Lori? You okay?"

"Yeah, my imagination's running wild, or I'm homesick, or crazy, or about to drop dead in exhaustion. I've been hauling boxes upstairs all day. My legs are rubber." I take a deep breath. There's a strange new scent in the room, like — what? Like the smoky smell of fired caps from the cowboy gun Randy used to have.

"I see him now," Randy whispers grimly. "Right behind you. Gertie there with you?"

"Downstairs, on the sleeping porch." I rub my thumb over the laptop's camera aperture, wondering if a smudged lens is to blame. But no, I see the figure again.

Limp dark hair curls over his brow. The rest of his hair is under a soldier's cap. This cap, his uniform, they're not like anything I've seen in real life. They're older, blue-black, trimmed in gold. A wide strap crosses his chest. He stares at me with those sad, unblinking eyes. Dad had mentioned that Gettysburg locals dress up to reenact the big battle. That must be who he is. But how did he get in my *room*? Why's he so silent, so . . . there but not there?

Randy shouts, "Don't make a move, mister. I can identify you if you so much as touch a hair on my sister's head. Lori, get out of that room pronto."

I turn slowly toward the image, ice water trickling through my veins. I reach for my nearby softball bat, and lock my hands around it. I could thwack him and do mortal damage. I crouch in my softball catcher's stance, ready to spring.

And feel totally idiotic, because the room is empty.

"He's gone," I tell my brother.

"At least move around the room again," Randy says. "Show me what you see on camera. I'll stay with you."

The screen light illuminates dark spots on the gloomy walls, and I search under the bed, in the wardrobe, behind the cartons and the heavy drapes over the six windows around the room.

"The door's locked from the inside; the windows are

locked. There's no way for anyone to get in or out of here," I whisper.

Does *he* hear me, whoever he is?

"We both saw·him, didn't we, Randy?" I ask.

I think back to when I was fourteen, when, after a Phillies game, I saw Great-Grandpa Tunis belt out, "Take Me Out to the Ball Game." The thing is, Great-Grandpa Tunis had died of a heart attack two years before that time. My own heart seizes now, and I remember the dead boy in the crystal ball. Randy doesn't know about any of those eerie things.

"I'm not sure now," Randy murmurs. "I just woke from a deep sleep in the middle of a dream. I haven't had a real shower in six days because the plumbing's on the fritz, and you, you're stressed out in the new digs. Let's just chalk it up to fatigue and overactive imaginations. Skype me tomorrow morning. Clearer heads — that'll work better. Scratch that; I may be gone a couple days." He yawns again, and I feel stupid and guilty for the whole ridiculous — what? — shared hallucination? So I blow Randy a kiss, log out of Skype, and close the laptop.

I'm dog tired, but the bed's mountain high with clothes. I knee my way up and crawl under the pile to warm up — the temperature's definitely dropped — and to steady my racing heart. No sheets on the bed yet, not even a mattress pad. It doesn't matter, because I don't dare go to sleep. I sit up straight against the headboard, still holding my softball bat, eyes darting around the tower room that's dusk dark even with all the lights on. I should have claimed a room downstairs, a regular square room.

The smoky smell intensifies. I look around, seeking out a candle left over from the last occupants, or a match or old cigarette under the bed. Nothing.

There's no one in the room, I tell myself. I'm starting to drift in that foggy trance between awake and asleep. I pinch my arm and check that the bat's close enough that I can grab it and swing. I have to stay vigilant all night. I whisper into the empty room, "Who are you? Why are you here?" I'm not really scared now, because I'm not picking up threatening vibes. I'm more curious than anything, willing myself to stay up.

"Lorelei Cordelia."

My head snaps up, startling me awake, though I was sure I hadn't slept a wink.

My eyes dart around the room.

"Lorelei Cordelia," the soft voice says again. I must be dreaming. I blink the sleep away, and hear it again.

It has to be Dad. He's the only one who calls me Lorelei. He came to tuck me in on my first night here, just like he used to

when I was little. Sweet and totally explainable. It's just that I
didn't see him when he came and left, because I'd fallen asleep.
Sure, that's it.

But my door is locked. From the inside. Meaning someone
inside my room called my name, and he's still here. Somewhere.

3

I MUST HAVE fallen asleep again, because I'm splayed out on my bare mattress, which has pocked my back with button indentations. I look like an alien from the planet Trypchrd, where button pocks are considered beauty marks.

As I sit up, a menacing feeling churns between my heart and my stomach, the kind you get when you know something's wrong, but you can't remember what it is yet.

And then it hits me. Someone was, is, in my room. My eyes zoom around the circular space and up to the high ceiling, which is bordered with blue plaster cherubs. More cherubs hang from the tarnished chandelier. I'm half expecting that strange image, the soldier I saw, or imagined, or dreamed, to be hovering above me, too.

But I sense that I'm totally alone now. My heart slows to a normal *lub-dub*. I'm in yesterday's wrinkled jeans and T-shirt, not in my usual PJ boxers and tee. My teeth feel like peach fuzz and I seriously need a shower.

It's still morning-cool in my room. If I can get my legs wheeling, I'll go for a run before the oppressive heat drags the day down. By noon my room will be a sauna, since there's no A/C up here. Unless the temperature dives suddenly, the way it did last night.

Wait a minute. Where's my bat? Did it fall out of my hand while I was sleeping? I paw through the graveyard of shirts and pants and hoodies and hangers and last winter's parka. No bat. I maneuver off the bed and look around the room. Maybe it rolled under my desk. Nope, I can see it's not there.

What actually happened last night? *Lorelei Cordelia.* I'm sure I heard my name, clear as wind chimes. Was it a dream? No, I'm *really* sure someone was in my room. Randy saw him, too. I rub my eyes until they sting.

The wobbly tower of boxes taunts me. Everything's waiting to be unpacked, and I'll have to put the extra stuff up in the attic. I've never lived in a house with an attic. I've never lived in a house, period, and just the thought of an attic is a little unnerving. I picture bats (the flying kind), dust balls, mice trails, dead roaches, something alive crouching in a dark corner. Or not alive. My imagination's on overdrive after last night's weird encounter.

Get a grip! I walk over to one of the windows. The heavy brocade drapes have a pattern of prissy Shakespeare people. Men in tights. Ick. When I peel back a drape, sunlight floods the grim room and evaporates last night's mystery like morning dew. Again I'm practically blinded by the immense emerald lawn down below. Old Dryden, the gardener, is bent over his flowers, like he hasn't moved since yesterday. Or maybe he's actually a lawn ornament.

Here comes an engine sputtering up the driveway. Sounds like Jocelyn's Ford Ranger pickup. But no, it's a souped-up rusty Camaro, as yellow as a taxi, riding on tires big enough for a tractor. It's a disaster of a car, from which that boy Evan Maxwell hops out. The engine keeps cranking a few seconds more. Evan opens the trunk and pulls out a Weedwacker, which he swings around his head like he's roping a raging bull. He's wearing a Dallas Cowboys T-shirt today, I see from way up here. I grab my glasses off my desk to inspect closer. His blond hair wisps over his eyes, and his jeans are holey at the knees. He and Old Dryden seem to be in an argument. I tug up the window, and it slides open silently like it's greased with butter. Evan's got a voice that carries. Probably has an ego to match.

"Dryden, my friend, get with the program. You look like your body made a U-turn. Scoliosis, man, and it's not getting any better the longer you bend over picking weeds. This Weedwacker, I'm telling you, it's the solution to all your problems."

"You're my problem," Old Dryden yells.

Evan squats to look up into Old Dryden's face. "You want to go through life like a pretzel?" He stands up and pets the Weedwacker. "Trust me, this little honey will save your life. Give it a test run."

Old Dryden waves him away. Evan switches on the Weedwacker, and it hums to life.

"Turn that thing off!" shouts Old Dryden. Then he mellows, noticing how efficient the spinning metal string is. "That how she goes?"

"Yup. Want to hold her?" The old guy backs away. Evan looks up and spots me. I freeze. The evil Weedwacker takes advantage of the moment, topples a whole bed of daffodils, and is moving robotically toward a rosebush.

"Argggggggg!" Old Dryden cries.

Evan cuts the motor. It dies a slow death, like his car, while he looks up and beams at me. Embarrassed, I duck down, then slowly rise again to check if he's gone. He's still staring up at my window, like Romeo gazing at Juliet, while Old Dryden mournfully caresses an armload of lopped-off daffodils.

"Hi, up there," Evan calls with a wave. "Me, again. We met yesterday." He hops on the second rung of a trellis under my window, but I'm still three stories above him. "Evan Maxwell, remember? Dryden's worthy assistant."

"Hi." I wave back.

"He's no such," Old Dryden protests.

"Come on, you're breaking my heart, man."

"Mow the lawn, that's it. Don't you ever come near my flowers again, not with that mechanical monster."

Evan jumps down and strides toward the shed, where I'm guessing the lawn mower is parked. He's kind of self-impressed, or else he's trying real hard to impress me. But why would he care? He's cuter than Danny Bartoli, and Danny never even noticed me.

Backing away from the window, I knock over a box, and all my desk stuff spills out — pens, pencils, staplers, Tootsie Pops, and scruffy softballs from the last two summer leagues, plus my beautifully broken-in mitt and a million paper clips. Odd — I'm sure that box was taped shut last night.

I dump the rest of the box on the floor. My room looks ransacked by burglars.

A zillion staples fall out of their little Altoids tin. Something's missing; I sense it. I scramble through all the loose papers and old letters and a calendar from two years ago, the phone charger. Seeing what's there is a lot easier than figuring out what's not. What's missing? My address book's here, and the little leather notebook with all my passwords . . .

My journal, that's what's missing! Someone's stolen my private thoughts. How *dare* he!

Who?

A creepy wave radiates over me. I cross my arms over my waist, feeling naked even in my slept-in clothes.

What is happening in this strange room? Could Bertha Dryden be right about the house being haunted?

I have to talk to somebody, see a live and sympathetic face.

I power up my laptop and type out a quick e-mail to my brother.

LoriC@squareone.com
Let's set up a Skype time, Randy. Got a lot
to tell you.

No response. He's probably teaching. I want to call Jocelyn, but there's no cell phone reception at that horseback-riding camp where she's working. I message her.

LoriC@squareone.com
You online, Jos?

Nothing wings its way back to me.

Okay. Ping me when you get some
Wi-Fi time.

A good run with Gertie — that'll clear my cottony head.
But first, a shower. I turn to grab a towel and see my bat
propped up on the dresser.

I would never have put it there myself.

4

I TAKE A quick shower. Steam pours out when I open the bathroom door, clutching the short towel around my long body, and there's Evan Maxwell, unplugging computer cables for the carpet guys. As I dash past him, he turns lobster-red and mutters, "Sorry, didn't know you were in there." I am totally mortified, but not half as embarrassed as he is.

I change quickly into shorts, a T-shirt, and my running sneakers. I don't bother trying to put my contacts into my puffy-from-lack-of-sleep eyes.

As I open my door to head downstairs, I see the bunch of

maintenance men tearing up the carpeting on the stairs, like a bandage off a raw wound. I step carefully to avoid tripping over nailheads or splintery wood. Mom and Dad are supervising. I don't mention anything to them about what happened last night. They'd freak.

I find Gertie in the kitchen, where she's following Bertha around like a lovesick pup.

"Hey, Gertie Girl." She looks up as if she remembers me from her distant past and idly ambles toward me. I give her the old belly tickle, and her eyes light up. I'm winning her back. What a fair-weather friend Gertie's turning out to be. "Mrs. Dryden, I was wondering —"

"You call me Bertha. It's a sturdy, respectable name, not one of those froufrou names like Brandy or MacKenzie." She squints at me. "Say, you weren't wearing those glasses yesterday. I'd of remembered."

"Contacts, usually."

"Well, good thing. You know the old saying, 'Boys don't make passes at girls who wear glasses.'"

I try not to roll my eyes. "Oh, so that explains why I didn't go to the prom."

Not that either Jocelyn or I wanted to. Proms are so retro, suburban chic, extravagantly wasteful, and antifeminist. They do not have a place in a balanced ecosystem. I mean, look at all those strobe lights and glitter and crushed flowers and fuel-guzzling limos. Proms are antigreen to the max.

Also, we didn't have dates. So Jos and I went to see a musical. What could be greener than *Wicked*?

"You have a good night?" Bertha asks me. For a second I think she's asking about prom night, but no, she's staring at me with belligerent challenge. Suddenly, I wonder if it might have been Bertha who got into my room last night and messed up my things. Took my journal, even. She might have a master key for all the rooms. How do I ask without being insulting?

"So, I was wondering, Bertha," I begin hesitantly, "if you might have seen a journal I had in my room. Maybe it got mixed up with some of the house books or something."

"Am I the lost-and-found? You can see how busy I am. Your parents expect people will be checking in here in a few days. No, I haven't seen your blessed journal. Mighta been Charlotte. She's a sneaky snoop."

Charlotte, the cleaning girl, hasn't been here since we moved in. "Thanks. I'll check with her whenever she shows up," I say pointedly.

"The slacker's already four minutes late," Bertha grumbles.

"Maybe your watch is fast. Come on, Gertie."

My dog looks guilty abandoning Bertha, but she trots behind me.

It's already too hot to run. "Let's go down to the creek, Gertie."

There's nothing she loves more than jumping into a pond or pool on a hot summer day, so now she's racing ahead of me.

Coolspring Creek is really like a mini-river, much wider than I thought, but not so deep. It's got a lazy current rippling through it, and it's about the length of a football field until it reaches the end of our property in the woods, where it's dammed by fallen trees. Gertie throws me a *Can I?* glance, I nod, and she leaps in. She's a great swimmer, giving joyful meaning to dog-paddling.

Wish I'd thought to put my suit on. It's already proving to be a beastly hot day, and the water is so inviting. I take off my sneakers and sit, dangling my feet in the rambling stream. Heavenly. The creek's so pure and clean that I can see every movement of my face. I stick out my tongue, cross my eyes, suck in my cheeks.

Then I see another face.

A handsome, familiar one. The same face I saw in the Skype video feed.

I whip around, and there's no one behind me. What is the *story* here? Am I going crazy? I feel a . . . how do I describe it? A thickening of the air behind me. Dumb, Lori. What are you thinking? Air isn't thick.

Okay, a density? A vibration? It's like a magnet has drawn a zillion molecules into something invisible. Something that has a face that reflects in the water.

"Who are you?" I whisper, not that I expect an answer. "Are you a Battle reenactor?"

Silence.

"Who are you?" I repeat. "Because you're really spooking me."

And then I hear it: a reply, hovering in the air just over my head.

"I am Na-than-iel-Pierce."

My imagination playing tricks again? I whistle for Gertie to come for protection. She scrambles out of the creek and shakes off water in a wide arc. The reflection in the creek disappears as the air behind me slackens off. Whoever it is doesn't like to get wet, or doesn't like dogs. Gertie sniffs the ground and yelps a little, but she's no guard dog, just curious.

"Is that your name?" I call out, still looking in the creek. "Nathaniel Pierce? Why are you doing this to me? Tell me right now."

No answer. Well, did I expect someone who isn't there to answer? But he *did* give me his name, and he knows mine.

Holding Gertie's wet body like a shield, I get real brave. "Okay, if you're not a reenactor, if you're a ghost or something —

I can't believe I'm saying this — you might as well let me see you. This hide-and-seek isn't working for me."

The dense air shimmers. Right in front of my eyes, the molecules — or whatever — form themselves into a shadowy image. A young man, maybe two years older than I am, wearing that same blue visor cap. For one crazy moment I think he's my mirror reflection. I reach up to see if there's a cap on my head.

He's still in that ragged military uniform, which maybe used to be navy blue, and one scuffed boot. The other foot's bound in filthy rags. His eyes capture me; obsidian-black pools. His lips move, but no sound comes out. Is he mute? Am I deaf?

Gertie sits peacefully on my lap, soaking me to the skin. She doesn't seem to see the boy at all. This is weird beyond disturbing, and yet something tells me it's okay, that I've been down this road before.

"Why are you here, Nathaniel Pierce?"

Gertie looks up, but realizes I'm not talking to her.

The soldier's heard me. He shakes his head from side to side, me following those black eyes. He turns all the way around. That's when I see the torn fabric and dried blood of a gaping hole in the middle of his back. As if someone had aimed for his heart.

My own heart thuds, then sinks. Ever since the crystal-ball scare, I've tried to be a rational person, so I scan through possibilities. Theory One: He's really that gardener kid, Evan, in a wig and vintage uniform, playing a nasty trick on me. Evan seems like the kind who'll do anything for attention.

But no, the truth's in the eyes. This guy has those black, mesmerizing ones. And — whatever he is — he sends a warm feeling through me. My face flushes, as though there's a strong tug between us. The lawn-mower guy just makes me smile at his cute arrogance.

Theory Two: Nathaniel Pierce is a ghost, and I knew him in a past life. How bizarre is that? I don't believe in reincarnation. This is my first time around, for sure, and my last. Come on, if I'd lived before, wouldn't I have picked someplace more exotic for my next life than Gettysburg, Pennsylvania? I mean, really.

Okay, new theory. Maybe he's just a disturbance in the atmosphere. Weather patterns can do all kinds of crazy things, right?

Yeah, but what about the wound in his back? I ask myself.

Just then, he turns around and hands me something. I blink, realizing what it is. *My diary!*

"You read my private thoughts!" I snap, my fury erasing my uncertainty about this apparition.

His eyes are haunting, unnerving. They're not just sad; they plead. He needs something from me. He clears his throat and says hoarsely, "Your diary . . . you don't write in it much, do you?"

"Only when the spirit moves me." Instantly I realize how ironic *that* is.

Our hands brush briefly. His smile is warm and doesn't jibe with those sad eyes. "Forgive me," he says. I'm not sure I'm ready to.

I take the diary and flip it open. No wonder he knew my full name — it's written there on the first page: *Lorelei Cordelia Chase.*

I flip to the last entry, about my farewell party. Danny Bartoli was there, so I'd detailed certain things about him: his short, curly hair; his broad shoulders; his favorite phrase, which is "catch ya after the fireworks," written seven times across the page. Oh! This is humiliating. I flip past more pages. Then I notice a page dog-eared, an old entry from my freshman year of high school. It's the one about the crystal ball, the dead boy from Delaware County.

I look up and my eyes meet Nathaniel Pierce's. He says, "I had to be sure you were the one."

I shoot back, "Which one? I don't know what you're talking

about, but I'll tell you this, Nathaniel Pierce, reading my journal is such an invasion."

His eyes narrow, as if he's puzzled. He's a soldier: *Invasion*
has a different meaning in the military. "Trampling on my private life," I explain, though my words are losing steam. He's
stirred me, charged my curiosity. "What do you want with
me?" I demand.

"I need your help to solve a murder."

"Oh, really? Who's the murder victim?" I ask sarcastically.

"I am."

His eyes flutter shut. Such long, dark eyelashes brush his
rough cheeks. Then, in a second, he's gone, and I suddenly feel
an overwhelming loneliness. My own, or his?

5

THIS IS TOO much for me to handle alone. I need to talk to Jocelyn. I shoot her a quick message, hoping for an immediate response.

LoriC@squareone.com
Hey, Jos, you there?

She writes back right away.

JocelynJ@squareone.com
here, hi. trying 2 cope w/snarky pre-pubescent horsey girls. if I think abt taking a camp counselor job next summer, slap me til I'm delirious. what's up?

I take a deep breath. Where do I start?

I think I met a ghost.

what?? Jocelyn types back after a split second. *we don't do those seances anymore, Lori.*

I know, I write back, my thoughts racing. But this seems different . . . real. He spoke to me. He wants me to solve his murder.

ur kidding me, right? what's he look like?

Dark, sad eyes, dark hair, ragtag blue uniform. I'm pretty sure there's a bullet hole in his back.

OMG! Jocelyn writes. I can't tell if she believes me or not, but before I can ask, she

writes, *hey. I have to go to riding practice.*
keep me posted!!

I leave my bedroom and stagger downstairs in a daze. I wonder if I should go back to the creek and try to find Nathaniel again. Or will he come find me? My parents have gone out to track down the nearest Home Depot. If they were here, would I tell them what was going on? I'm not sure.

In the front hall, I practically bump into a barefoot girl. Her high-top sneakers are clamped under her arm while she tries to tie a scarf around her wild chipmunk-brown hair. It's long enough to sit on. Ouch.

"Hi," she says to me. "I'm Charlotte. I'm late again, I know."

The grandfather clock in the hall is chiming the quarter hour — one of the few things I like about this house.

"Don't worry," I tell her. "Bertha's in the basement."

She smiles and drops her sneakers. "Didn't know you'd moved in already."

"I'm Lori, and yeah, we're here," I say with a sigh.

Charlotte nods. "So, you've met the darling Drydens."

"Charmers."

Charlotte's hopping on one foot while struggling to get her sock and shoe on the other. I move aside so she can plop down on the bottom step to complete the job.

"New carpeting, and so foresty green," she says, looking around. "I'll be vacuuming up green scraps and fibers for weeks." Her jeans are creamy-soft, thinned to nearly white in places, and her T-shirt hugs her roundish middle. A monkey grins on the front, with his arm stretched all the way around to her back like a hug.

"I'll help vacuum," I volunteer, eager for something to take my mind off Nathaniel. "Lots of hotel experience."

An uneasy look flashes across Charlotte's face and vanishes just as fast. "That'll be a change. I've done this house by myself for the past four years. Ever since I turned fifteen." She lifts the hem of her shirt and wipes a smudge off the wallpaper. "This house is putting me through school. I'll be a sophomore at the college, come fall. What about you?"

"One more year of high school," I mutter.

"Get Mrs. Whitmont for English. The other one, Engles, is hideous. Oh, and make sure you get your locker at the north end of the hall, away from the bathrooms." Charlotte wrinkles up her nose. "Smells emanate."

I like her easy, chattery way.

"Which room's yours?" she asks me, standing up.

"The round one, up top."

"You're living in the tower?" Charlotte looks horrified.

"There does seem to be something odd about it," I admit, the memory of last night making me shudder.

She frowns. "Like what?"

I don't know how to answer, so she says, "A spirit?"

My shock must show on my face. "I — I don't know," I stammer. "It sounds ridiculous. You probably don't believe in ghosts any more than I do."

"I believe, actually. Spirits are all around us," she says matter-of-factly. "I have to block them out. Sometimes humming works, or whistling." She treats me to a high-pitched version of the Seven Dwarfs' *Heigh-Ho, heigh-Ho, it's off to work we go.* "Listen, I have an idea. It's my night off from my other job. My boy-friend, Eddie, is busy working so I'm totally free. Why don't we take one of those ghost tours tonight? We'll meet at the tour place on Steinwehr, quarter to ten. By the time we're done, maybe you'll know whether what you saw in the tower room is a spirit for real or not." She walks over to the linen closet, reaching in for an armful of sheets. She says over her shoulder, "Some see spirits, some don't. Maybe you'll be one of the lucky ones."

Yes, but is it lucky to see them, or lucky not to? Guess I'll find out tonight. It'll be corny and over-the-top for sure. But in the back of my mind I'm hoping I'll encounter Nathaniel Pierce, since I don't know any other way to find him. And I think I do want to see him again.

The candlelight ghost tour looks like trick or treat. Murmuring clusters of ghost-walkers are padding around in the dark.

"Gee, I hope there are enough ghosts to go around," I joke.

Charlotte seems jittery. "Don't worry."

Our group is an edgy circle of people, some with cameras to capture the spirits on video. Heather, our guide, counts us and proclaims, "Oh, dear, thirteen, not an auspicious number." She wears a long hoop-skirted dress to make her look 1860ish. The dress sways over her red checkered Vans, which we're not supposed to see. Impossibly black, straight wig-hair hangs down her back, trailing to wispy ends. She is careful to remind us that there are no guarantees and no refunds. "Even if you don't have a single experience on this dark, moonless night of high promise."

It sounds silly, but it's fun, like the séances Jos and I used to do.

We each get a glow-stick bracelet, so we all look bile-green and ghoulish. We follow Heather's lantern, in which a single candle melts. The trick is to finish the walk before the candle's just a waxy puddle and we're all plunged into what Heather calls "the dark depths of despair such as some of our resident spirits experience."

No one is taking this seriously, although Charlotte looks greener than most of us.

We trudge up Steinwehr Avenue while Heather talks about the history of Gettysburg in a somber monotone so as not to disturb the spirits. She stops and lays her palm reverently on the ground. "In this very battlefield hundreds of soldiers lay wounded or dead." We peer into the dark abyss of grass made black by night. "Some hear their piteous moans."

What I hear is a car full of kids racing up the pike, horns blaring.

"Feel the breeze of passing spirits," Heather drones. "I implore you to engage all your senses. See, hear, smell, taste, touch the mysteries around you."

I listen, look, touch the grass, sniff at the air. Nothing.

Heather holds her lantern up to shoulder height so we can step around the breaks in the cement without stumbling into the gutter, and she leads us ghouls up the road. She has tales for just about every building. After a half hour, we come to Weinbrenner Creek. Suddenly the atmosphere changes and the hair stands up on the back of my neck and my arms. I interrupt Heather's script: "What happened here?"

She raises her lantern to highlight my face. Her look's intense, jarring.

"By July fourth, which wasn't yet a national holiday, the Battle had ended. It was not the end of misery in this town, where bodies of men and horses were strewn everywhere. Even more tragic were the wounded who waited for help."

"But what happened *here*?" I demand again, and Charlotte gives me an elbow to the ribs.

"Patience. I'm coming to that," Heather says. "Look down into the creek. Imagine four wounded soldiers writhing in agony. They're awaiting rescue to a field hospital, too weak, too torn apart, to get there on their own. A driving rain comes. It rains so torrentially that the summer-dry creek fills with flood waters. All four soldiers are washed away, drowned."

I gaze down at the tall grass waving in the breeze. A raw, searing grief shakes me to my bones. I rip off the ghoulish glow bracelet and drop it gently into the creek — flowers on a grave.

"I have to go home, right now," I whisper to Charlotte. This all feels suddenly too real to me.

"You can't do that," Charlotte hisses. "Next stop's the cemetery. That's the best part." She pats my arm to soothe me, and I'm wondering what on earth just happened. It's like a sudden storm surged through me, then passed almost as quickly.

Heather's lantern dances through the dark, then glows brighter as the moon slides behind a cloud. Heather leads us up the road toward the cemetery. Make that *cemeteries*, plural. Lucky Gettysburg, always obsessed with death, has two, right next to each other. There's Evergreen, where, according to Heather, the locals have been burying their dead since 1854. Good to know life and death happened here even before the Battle. And there are still plots available, the sign says. Wow, something to look forward to.

"Right next door," Heather tells us, "is the National Soldier's Cemetery where Lincoln gave his famous Gettysburg Address. But, sad to say, it's locked at night. Still, it's our good fortune that Evergreen has no locked gates, so, here we go!"

A shiver runs through me, which I try to hide from Charlotte. She tugs me through the open gates. Just inside there looms a statue that looks totally black in the dark.

"This is Elizabeth Thorn." Heather pours candlelight over the darkened bronze. "She and her husband ran the cemetery during the Civil War, but he was off soldiering in another state and wasn't a veteran of our local Battle. That left poor Elizabeth to do the work of two, and with a passel of young children, besides."

The statue captivates me. What was so special about this woman that they made a whole statue of her? She was obviously pregnant, and how often do you see a pregnant statue? I circle the whole figure and come back to the front to stare at her face so long that I lose track of the rest of the group, who've wandered deeper into the cemetery. Charlotte doubles back to pull me toward the others.

We walk over graves while Heather talks about the lives of the spirits. I've stopped listening, This place feels so eerie. The ground is an impenetrable black with headstones jutting upward, silvery white as the moon that slides in and out of the clouds.

"Should we be walking on these graves?" I ask Charlotte.

"They don't mind." She's humming quietly but doesn't seem upset, like a cemetery is her natural habitat, the way squirrels live in trees.

Heather says, "Ladies and gents, this concludes our tour. Come back tomorrow to visit the National Soldier's Cemetery. Of course, it's not as captivating in the light of day."

Her candle's just a stub now, barely poking its lit wick over the puddle of wax, and she's leading our crew toward the Evergreen gates. I stop suddenly and yank on Charlotte's shirt. The headstone in front of us is radiating heat. Charlotte nods her approval as I tentatively reach out and touch the granite for a second, then snap my hand back like it might get scorched. I can't see the name on the headstone because the moon has dipped below the horizon. But I know whose grave it is.

And then I see him materializing in front of the headstone, and my heart leaps to my throat.

"Nathaniel Pierce," I whisper, startling Charlotte, who says, "That's his name?"

Nathaniel sees that I'm not alone, and he vanishes, vaporizes, whatever.

Charlotte isn't at all surprised. "I've always wondered who he was," she whispers, "but he's never spoken to me. Handsome guy, isn't he? Wonder what his story is."

I'm stunned that Charlotte has seen Nathaniel, and I want to tell her everything. But at the same time, I sense that what Nathaniel has told me is private, somehow. He only wants me to know it.

Heather calls to us. "Girls? Come! We're walking back to our meeting place, and please be assured, pilgrims, that I wouldn't be insulted by a small gratuity. . . ."

Charlotte leans toward me. "She's a total phony, but your Nathaniel Pierce, he's the real thing."

6

IN THE DAYS after the ghost tour, I don't see Nathaniel again, and I don't know why. Did I do something to offend him? Has he turned to someone else? That would hurt.

I try Googling his name, but I come up with a million different hits, none of which seems to have anything to do with a Civil War–era ghost.

I have to put him out of my mind while we're hurrying to get the house ready for our first guests. The town's gone into hyperdrive for the upcoming Battle Days. People are renting out rooms in their homes. Restaurants push tables so close you can practically eat off your neighbor's plate. Excitement zings in the air. The Battle reenactors have started showing up on the streets.

"Those loonies, they take vacation days," Bertha tells me, repotting a massive red geranium in the downstairs parlor. "Every boss man in Adams County gives 'em off. But look at 'em. There's thousands. Horses, too. We don't have enough in all of Pennsylvania to fill the ranks on both sides, Rebs and Yanks both."

"Where do they come from, then?" I ask, polishing the wooden table, per Mom's instructions. Charlotte's busy cleaning the bathrooms, so I pitched in. "Like, imported imposters?"

"Those diehards, they take their uniforms out of mothballs and pour in from all over the US of A. They'd bawl like babies if they had to miss these first few days in July. The crazies want it the way it was back *when*, so folks gussy up in Civil War blues and grays and red britches, shooting at each other. Use to be a battleground, you know, blood running like a river. Musta been a sight to see, all right. Now it just pays good."

That Bertha — she's all heart.

You wouldn't think so many able-bodied men would be available to replay the Civil War like it's a video-game simulation. It flits through my mind again that Nathaniel might just be one of those reenactors playing a trick on me.

No. Randy saw him. Charlotte saw him, too, and recognized him, and then saw him vanish into thin air. I'm not crazy, I'm not dreaming, but I don't know how to label what it is I am. Mesmerized? Possessed? Whatever it is, it frightens me and at the same time thrills me.

Bertha's carrying on, but I'm not paying attention. She's using a paring knife to clean potting soil out from under her jagged nails. Vaguely I hear her say, "You know about that red flag hanging over the front door?"

"Evan told me about it," I reply. "The red flag signifies this once was a field hospital."

"Mr. Know-it-All. Bet he didn't tell you the rest."

My ears perk up.

"The original building, it turned to ashy rubble around 1872, and it wasn't rebuilt until the Carmodys came along six years later. The Carmodys had it until the turn of the century — twentieth, that is — and then the next folks changed the name to Coolspring Inn, Coolspring being the original name, back when."

"Fascinating." I zone out, wondering how to conjure up Nathaniel when I want to see him.

"Doesn't matter what you call it," Bertha says, "'cause on quiet nights, you can still hear the screams of the soldiers having their arms and legs cut off. Without an anesthetic. Another reason I won't stay in this house after midnight."

I mentally inventory Nathaniel's arms and legs, wondering if he suffered any losses. He has only one boot. The other foot's covered in heavy rags. I hope there's truly a foot in there.

"Looks like I spilled potting soil on this throw rug. Mind taking it out and giving it a good pounding?"

I'm glad to, to get away from Bertha.

Outside, Evan's mowing the lawn to within an inch of its life. He rides that mower like he's mounted on a mighty steed.

"Come on up," he offers, patting the seat beside him.

"Sorry, I'm swamped," I say, blushing. "The first guests arrive this afternoon."

"I can promise you a trip you'll never forget, cruising the grounds at a record-breaking three miles per. No?" He shrugs, grinning. "Your loss. Hey, tell your parents that I checked out the house computers. Everything's purring, but they should call if there are any problems. Or you can call."

Is he flirting with me, or is it my imagination? I can't trust myself these days. I wave to him and walk away just as Bertha comes out with the geranium pot.

"Never trusted that boy," she mutters, watching Evan as he rides off on the mower.

"Your husband doesn't think much of him, either," I reply. Then I realize I haven't seen Old Dryden's cheery face today. "Where *is* your husband?" I ask out of curiosity.

"He's out back soaking his flower beds good so he can take off the next four days," Bertha replies. "He always sleeps 'round the clock through the Battle Days. Loves the lullaby sound of gunfire, even if they're just blanks. I tell you, it takes all kinds."

It's two thirty in the afternoon, and the first guests will be arriving at three. Dad is running around troubleshooting the leaks and squeaks that keep popping up all over the house.

"We are hemorrhaging money, Miriam. M-o-n-e-y," he cries.

Mom reassures him, "We have a full house for the Battle commemoration, and lots of nice reservations through the rest of the summer. We'll come out okay, Vernon, you'll see."

"Hope so," Dad mutters. "And I promise you, Miriam, as soon as we see some headway, more coming in than bleeding out, Bertha will be ancient history."

Which I think is funny, because this whole place is about history; history of the living and history of the dead.

I shower quickly before the guests arrive. Summers in

Philly always meant softball games, with me as catcher and our team, the Liberty Bells, trouncing toward the league championship. I sure miss those games. Softball, that was righteous sweat; this is just grime and humidity grit.

I change into a light sundress, but then decide to find a newer pair of sandals up in the attic. I lift the ceiling door into the attic — and Nathaniel's there, waiting for me. Not a shimmery vision like lake water, but three-dimensional, solid, and . . . alive.

"I thought you'd never come," he says.

It takes me a minute to get my bearings, and then I respond.

"Me? You're the one who's a no-show, the one who does the vanishing act. I'm just a mere mortal."

Nathaniel's dark eyes crinkle with a smile. "I like your zest," he says. "You're feisty."

"I can't tell, is that a compliment?"

"Most certainly." His eyes lock on mine. "Lorelei." There's a pause, and then he adds, "Forgive me. I should have asked you, do you want me to call you Lorelei or something else? I couldn't tell from your diary."

"Lori," I reply.

"Lori. Lori." He rolls my name over his tongue. It's never sounded so sweet. "I prefer Lorelei. Would you mind? It's a timeless name."

I surprise myself by nodding. I never like it too much when my dad uses that old-fashioned name, but it sounds so much better on Nathaniel's lips. "That's fine," I tell him.

Nathaniel gives a fleeting smile, but then his eyes fill with sorrow. "I need your help, Lorelei."

"What can I do?" I ask.

He sits on a trunk stuffed with winter bedding and hangs his head. His felt cap falls to the floor. I'm struck by how dark and wavy his hair is, trailing down his elegant neck. I want to tuck that beautiful hair behind his ears, trace my fingers along the conch folds of his ears. He picks up the cap and begins to twist it. Then he gazes at me, sending chills and warmth through me at once.

"Time is slipping away," he responds. "I have only until midnight on the third of July."

"What's the rush?" I'm just starting to feel comfortable with him, especially now that he's solid enough for me to touch. Not that I'm ready to reach out and do that yet.

"It's hard to explain," he says softly. "I come here every year during the Battle Days, and when they end, I return to — you would think of it as oblivion, but it's more like hibernation. Bears hibernate; spirits also."

I bite my lip, considering. "Is it sort of suspended animation?"

"Yes, that describes it well. When I'm animated, as I am now, with you, solid and sinewy, I don't want to return to that other fleshless world. But I have no choice. It's my fate."

"I don't believe that. People can change if they want to."
Look how much I've changed in just a few days, I'm thinking. *Here I am, talking with a ghost.*

He shakes his head slowly and rubs his hand down his neck, his arm. "How do you stand it, how quickly time passes in bodily form?"

I pinch the flesh of my arms. "This is the only form I've ever had. It's impossible to answer your question."

"Never mind then; just listen." Now his words come in hurried bursts. "You are my only chance. I've waited months, years, decades, a century and a half."

I sit down on a pillow across from him. "Waited for what, Nathaniel? Tell me."

"Answers to what happened to me, back then, during the Battle." He takes a breath. "I already told you I was murdered."

"Yes, but . . ." I'm not sure how to phrase this next part. "How's dying in battle the same as murder?"

"Let me explain," Nathaniel says, leaning forward. "On the third battle day, I had a bayonet stab wound to my shoulder and was ordered to the infirmary. Doctors and nurses, mostly civilian volunteers from Gettysburg, they were all doing what they could for so many wounded, so fast. Sometimes just washing a soldier's face with cool water, maybe giving him a shot of something strong to ease the pain, or calling for a chaplain. Some wounded just lay on the grass, on bare wood, on dirt floors. I was one of the lucky ones. I had a stretcher, but I rolled off to make room for a boy from Indiana. Told him, 'Be strong, soldier. You'll be back home under a sycamore in no time,' but it was a lie. I knew he wouldn't make it through the night. I pressed a rag to my own shoulder. In a minute it was soaked with blood."

Nathaniel gasps, shudders, reliving the intense pain and shock, as fresh this moment as it was all those years ago. He topples forward. I catch his head in my hands and slowly lift it, slowly raise his shoulders — feel the ripple of the stab wound at his shoulder — until he's sitting upright again. It's amazing to be able to touch him — solid and warm and real.

"At times, in this bodily form, the pain overwhelms me," he says in a feverish whisper.

I sit beside him on the trunk now. I wait for the years and pain to pass until he comes back to me. Like my brother Randy and me, so close and yet four thousand miles apart, Nathaniel and I sit together, separated by a hundred and fifty years.

Finally I sense his body relaxing, the pain ebbing away, and

I know that this is a scene I will replay a thousand times in my memory, in my dreams. I'm choking on the memory of the future.

"Let me open the window. I can hardly breathe," I say. I crank the window open, relieved to feel a breeze flutter past me and to smell earthy life outside. "Better, don't you think?"

"I don't need air, or food, or water, or sleep. What I need is your help, Lorelei."

His tone makes me uneasy, as if he's about to say something I'll regret hearing. My impulse is to silence him, to keep everything just the way it is. But I can't. Something about him tugs at my heart. I sit back down on the trunk by his side.

"So, the next day you went back into battle?" I ask.

"No, I did not, for you see, that night I was shot in the back. Murdered by someone I never saw."

Stunned, I lock my hands over my racing heart. "So, you really meant it? That you were murdered?"

"As sure as you're sitting here with me today. I know now that you are the one I've waited for, the one always meant to find out the truth about who murdered me. You see things others do not see. The boy in the tree — I read about it in your diary," he reminds me. Like I could forget?

"Nobody else knows about that." After a long pause that he patiently waits through, I say, "Okay, where do we start?"

"You won't understand my death until you know about my life. But I can't talk anymore now. This corporeal form won't hold much longer."

"Wait! You can't leave me hanging this way, and I refuse to watch you fade away from me again," I say, stamping my foot.

He flashes me a thin smile. "Feisty, as I said. All right, then, Lorelei, you be the first to leave this time." He pulls a watch on a chain out of his pocket. It's rusted, and the crystal is broken. "The old thing hasn't ticked in a hundred years, but looking at it's a habit. Doesn't matter. I can tell what time it is by the sun. Let us meet here tomorrow, after your noon meal."

I nod and turn away, frustrated and still a bit in shock from our conversation. I clutch the handle on the cutout door that's both the attic floor and the ceiling below. Lifting the door, I start down the steps. My mistake is turning around to see him. He is already not there.

7

I'M SHAKING AS I return to my room and slip on my old flip-flops. I realize it's a decent hour in Ghana, and I have just enough time for a quick Skype with my brother.

I log on, and reach him. It's a relief to see his face pop up, wearing a big smile.

"How you holding up out there in the boonies?" he asks me. "No more mysterious night visitors?"

How do I answer without making him think I've gone totally into loonyland?

"Um, Randy? It's possible that this house is . . ."

"What, possessed? Dad phoned me last night and said that as soon as he troubleshoots one problem, something else breaks down."

"Besides that. The house might be — and don't start yelling — haunted."

I expect him to give me that head-tilted *Ya gotta be kidding* look, but instead he says, "Ever hear of the *kalunga* line?"

"Sounds like a dance you do at weddings."

"Not quite. It's a tradition among the Kikongo people here in West Africa. It means the threshold between worlds."

A ripple of recognition zips through me. "Worlds as in living and dead?"

"You got it, sis. People here believe that after death the soul travels the path of the sun as it sets in the west. A few hundred years ago, I'm talking pre-Gettysburg, West Africans kidnapped as slaves believed that the *kalunga* line was under the Atlantic Ocean, because the living became the dead when they got to the US as slaves." He pauses for a long time, studying me. "You still there, Lori? I see you, but the audio's dead."

I've just been silent, taking everything in. I blink at my brother. "You know the guy you saw the other night on Skype?"

"Yeah, but we were both wiped out that night, seeing things."

"He's been around a few more times, Randy."

My brother's shoulders rise and sink slowly. "And?"

"He's a dead soldier, and I've been talking to him." I swallow, watching my brother's stunned reaction. "So I guess you could say I'm hanging on the *kalunga* line, and to tell you the truth, it doesn't feel all that weird anymore." I'm not ready to tell Randy about my feelings toward Nathaniel. Or about his murder.

"Mom and Dad know about this?" he demands.

"You think I'd clue them in? No way! Mom would scuttle me off to a shrink, and Dad would go totally ballistic."

"Should I be worrying, Lori?"

Good question. "Not yet. Just stay tuned. I may have lots more to tell."

Randy nods, looking concerned. "I'm standing by. If you need me, just whistle. On second thought, there's a taboo here in Ghana: Don't whistle at night, and don't touch iguanas."

"Not a problem, since when it's night here, it's tomorrow there, and if there were iguanas strutting around at Coolspring Inn, Gertie would have them for lunch. A bunch of guests arrive in a few minutes. Full house for the next five days."

"Better keep your dead soldier under wraps. He could scare away the customers."

"I'm not letting him anywhere near them," I promise, but I know I have no control over Nathaniel Pierce.

• • •

Mr. and Mrs. Rodney Durning are the first guests to arrive. Mom's breathless from the frantic preparations, but when she greets the Durnings she's oozing cheer.

"Welcome, welcome! It's so nice to have you at the newly restored Coolspring Inn," she chirps, guiding them into her reception area in the parlor, where they *ooh* and *aah* over all the genuine fake replicas. Mr. Durning is squinting at a framed wall map from way back in 1860.

His wife says, "I read on the Internet that all these inns are haunted. Are they, truly?"

I cough into my fist.

Mom smiles like the Mona Lisa.

"You won't say, will you?" Mrs. Durning chuckles. "Well, I would sure like to experience a spirit or two, wouldn't you, Rodney?"

"Yeah, sure. How many you got staying here tonight?" he asks Mom.

"Spirits?" Mom asks playfully. "Too many to count. People, twelve, including my family." She turns to an elderly couple who just came in.

"We're the Crandalls!" the husband booms, as if he's announcing a circus act.

Mom seems a little frazzled and whispers to me, "Can these old folks make it up the stairs?" To them, she says, "So, we have you in the General Robert E. Lee room, second floor."

"Isn't he a Confederate?" asks Mrs. Crandall.

"And a great general and hero," Mom adds.

Mr. Crandall is not to be pacified. "The man lost the war. We are not staying in a loser's room."

It's not like General Lee actually *slept* in the room.

"Oh, dear," Mom says under her breath.

"I suppose we can switch you," Dad pipes up from behind the computer at the check-in desk. "Let's see. The only Union room that's not yet assigned is General Buford, but he's on the third floor."

Mrs. Crandall's eyes shift to the long, green staircase, and her husband says, "Come, Mother. Up we go to Buford. Tallyho!"

I tap my foot impatiently. Once all the guests are assigned their generals, I decide, I'll slip out of the house. Earlier that day, I'd noticed that half the yellow school buses in Pennsylvania have been commandeered, along with the Freedom Transit local trolleys, to carry tourists to the various points around Gettysburg. Every third building has a plaque declaring it official/original something-or-other, like the Tillie Pierce House, which the Lincoln Line goes right past. That's got to be my first stop. Maybe Tillie was Nathaniel's sister or mother, and someone at the house can tell me about him. I know, I'm obsessed.

The next guest to arrive is a woman shouldering a canvas bag stuffed with books. An orange extension cord dangles to the floor.

"You do have free Wi-Fi in the rooms, do you not?" she asks Dad. "The brochure said."

"Of course, Ms. Wilhoit. You requested a room with a large desk and good lighting. That would be General Jeb Stuart, on the third floor."

"Superb. I will need very little. You'll often see a Do Not Disturb sign on my door, in which case please just leave clean towels outside my room. I came here to work on my novel about Gettysburg, and I work at odd hours."

I step behind Dad to see the notes he's made on the computer. Wow, Amelia Wilhoit's a famous historical-romance novelist with seventeen books to her name. How cool. Maybe we'll turn up as characters in her next novel. I do see that she has plenty of books on Gettysburg in her bag. I give her my best profile as I lift her heavy-duty printer box.

So, we're now officially innkeepers. I hope Nathaniel Pierce doesn't mind our guests swarming around in his space. Maybe he'll materialize to welcome some of the travelers. An odd pang of jealousy darts through me. Nathaniel Pierce is *my* ghost, not theirs.

How bizarre is it that I'm even thinking that way?

After I've deposited Ms. Wilhoit's printer in her room, I bump into Charlotte in the hall. She's just put carnation sachets in all the guest-room drawers.

Should I mention Nathaniel? She hasn't said a word about the ghost tour, and she seems distracted now. I know she's rushing to get to her other job.

"Charlotte? Quick question." She stops to smile at me. "The guy you saw at the cemetery?" I whisper. "You know who I'm talking about?"

Her smile falters for a second. "Nathaniel, you said his name was? What about him?"

"*Anything* about him. He keeps popping up to talk to me but he's being mysterious. You said you've seen him before."

"And lots of others." She thrusts a sachet into my hands. "He needs something from you, Lori, if he's showing up to talk to you all the time. Find out what it is." Then she runs down the stairs, leaving me sniffing the sachet. I get the feeling she really doesn't want to talk about this, and that leaves me wondering if she knows something about Nathaniel that she's not telling me.

• • •

Tillie Pierce's house was already standing on Baltimore Street in 1863, but now it's a B&B. No vacancy. Everybody has to make a buck, right? In the front parlor there are about a million copies of her book for sale. It's called *What a Girl Saw and Heard of the Battle*. Maybe I ought to buy a copy. Sixteen dollars? Forget it.

A jingle of a ceramic bell on the book table brings a small woman out of the back room. She's wearing a swaying 1860s dress. I'm glad Mom doesn't make us dress like Civil War throwbacks.

"Oh, hello! You're the daughter of that new couple running Coolspring Inn," she says, clapping her hands as if she's smashing gnats.

Word gets around fast in this outpost. Is my picture up in the post office? "Yes, I'm Lori Chase. I was wondering about the girl who used to live here."

"Our Tillie — well, really, Matilda." She scoops up one of the little black books and holds it up to shoulder level like show-and-tell in kindergarten.

"I'll have to read the book one of these days."

Disappointed, the woman lays it facedown. No sale.

"I was wondering," I go on, "if Tillie is related to a Civil War soldier who fought here in the battle, someone named Nathaniel Pierce. Maybe he was her brother?" Please don't make him her *husband*!

"Our Tillie was a remarkable girl, from a well-to-do family by 1863 standards. Her father was a butcher; meat was dear in those days. Nowadays, well, we're all vegetarians. Nathaniel. Hmm. No, her brothers were William and James, and to my knowledge, the family had no soldiers in our famous Battle."

Around town, the Battle is always spoken of with a capital *B*.

"They did shelter five Union soldiers here when the house was surrounded by Confederates, but no kin, no Pierces. Have you been to the soldiers' cemetery to find your gentleman? Do you know his regiment? The state he comes from? Which day of the Battle he fell?"

"No, no, and no." I wish I did.

"Do you know *anything* about the man?" She eyes me skeptically. "What brings you to this soldier?"

My lips must look bloodless the way they're tucked into my teeth, so she draws her own conclusion. "Ah, I understand. He's reached you from the Other Realm. Godspeed."

As I turn to go, I realize it's not just Charlotte. Everyone in this town seems to believe in ghosts.

8

EARLY THE MORNING of June 30, I open the drapes to dispel last night's gloom. When I glance down at the lawn, parked right in front of the house is Jocelyn's fire-engine red pickup. Could it be?

I nearly leap all the way down the stairs to find her asleep in one of the porch rockers, with her feet up on the railing.

"Jocelyn! What're you doing here? You're supposed to be up in the Poconos with the horsey girls."

Rubbing sleep out of her eyes, she says, "I told them I

needed a day off 'cause my mom was getting married. They totally believed me. I left at midnight. Only took me four hours, and I have to be back by five o'clock today." She unravels her slumped body, and we throw our arms around each other. My ring gets tangled in her long, dark braids.

"Okay," she says, pulling back. "Where *is* your ghost?"

I glance around to make sure no one's heard her. Then I whisper, "It's not like I can just snap my fingers and Nathaniel appears like a genie."

She's thoughtful a moment, then, "He isn't *really* here anyway, is he? I mean, physically?"

Is he? How to answer? "I was able to touch him . . ." I say, and I feel myself blushing.

"Lorelei Cordelia," Jocelyn whispers, widening her eyes. "Are you falling for a ghost?"

"What? No. I don't know!" I snap. I realize I haven't thought about Danny Bartoli in days. "Besides, what do you know about love?" I challenge.

Jocelyn smiles. "I met someone at camp."

"You never said!"

"Hunh-uh. I was afraid the whole thing would curdle if I told. Cyberspace is toxic. Anyway, it didn't curdle. Jude's still sweet and fresh. Get this: He's a horse whisperer. Swear to God."

"That's wonderful," I tell her, and I feel a pang of envy. Wouldn't it be easier if I could fall for a flesh-and-blood boy? If I really am falling for Nathaniel, that is.

"The best news is, he only lives an hour away from us. From me. You live here, I guess." She looks around at *here*, and I see it through her eyes — a mellow, rambling house cloaked in history and mystery. "Wow, Lori, it's just like you described. Old and creepy. I like, I like. This would have been a fabulous place to do our séances, yes? I don't remember why we stopped doing them, do you?"

"Vaguely," I lie. Some things you don't tell even your best friend.

I usher Jocelyn in for breakfast, but Hannah has just pulled the muffins out of the oven, so she shoos us away. Gertie and I show Jocelyn the spooky basement, the attic, the shed, the creek, and finally, my tower room. We yammer like magpies, and I tell her everything I know about Nathaniel.

"What's great about you, Jos, is that you don't think it's weird that I'm communicating with a spirit who was killed — murdered — in 1863," I say as we sit in my room.

"Weird? Far from! It's totally the coolest thing."

I don't feel *quite* that way, but it is exciting. Jocelyn says she's starving, so we go downstairs for some of Hannah's cranberry muffins. Mom and Dad come out to say hello to Jocelyn just as the other guests start to wake up and emerge for breakfast.

Before long, Jocelyn has to sputter back to the Poconos in her leaky-tank pickup. I watch her go from my bedroom window, feeling melancholy. It's been so good to have her here for a few hours. So normal, if there's such a thing anymore.

Mom *ding-a-ling*s the parlor bell that calls me downstairs to greet the McLean family, from Cottonwood Falls, Iowa. They're a mom, a dad, two sons, and a Chihuahua named Brownie. Gertie's caught a whiff of the dog, and she's one happy pup. She's been lonesome, especially for males of the Chihuahua persuasion.

I gallop down the stairs with an armload of monogrammed towels that fly out of my hands when I bump headlong into Bertha.

"You being chased by wolves?" she snaps.

"Why, are they loose in here?"

"Awoooooool," Evan howls from the computer in the downstairs hall, where he's been designing a new website for the inn.

I'm gripped by a sudden idea. "Listen, I need to ask you something, Bertha. You can answer, too, Evan."

"I'm an afterthought," he pipes up. "Great for the male ego."

"I'll answer if it suits me," Bertha says. Her flowery peasant skirt is cinched at the waist and skims her swollen ankles.

"You two know the ropes around here," I say, glancing from one to the other. "It has to do with . . . ghost legend."

"It's not legend, missy; it's money-on-the-nose fact."

Evan rolls his eyes behind Bertha and hits a few keys dramatically.

"Okay," I say, not wanting to let on to Bertha that I fully agree with her. "But how can ghosts take on human form?"

"They're human, same as you and me."

Evan mouths, *That's a matter of opinion.*

Can I get through this with a straight face? "I mean, instead of appearing as shimmery, shadowy, see-throughy images or balls of light and energy. What about when they . . . solidify?"

"Like ice, you mean?" Bertha asks.

"Or real bodies?" Evan pantomimes a He-Man muscle and then a classic wavy female shape, but he drops his arms when Bertha turns toward him.

She scratches her head, loosening her shambles of a bun. "Mostly it's invisible beings hanging around behind you." She turns and glares at Evan. "Or a door opening or slamming — *wham!* — when you're not expecting it. Lord-a-mercy, it scares the living daylights outta you. Sometimes you gotta watch for dishes and such floating through the air" — Evan tosses a piece of paper like a Frisbee — "unless they're weighted down good, and even then. Ghosts are powerful things, even if they're all just puffs of air. But turning solid and all? No, never heard of that, no."

Is Nathaniel always going to be mostly air and mist, only solid for a few fleeting moments?

"Well, now, hold your horses," Bertha is saying. "I'm thinking how some tell about spirits that take on animal forms, coyotes and eagles and such. Cats, sometimes."

Evan says, "Lions and tigers and bears, oh my!"

He's kind of annoying, but also funny. Still, I can't lose my focus. "But not people?" I press on.

"Missy, you've seen too many movies about dead bodies that weren't dead. Ever see *Cape Fear*, with that Robert De Niro actor fella? He kept not staying dead about a dozen times."

"Guess I missed that Golden Oldie," I murmur.

"Too bad. It was a nail-biter." Bertha smirks; two bottom teeth are missing, one on each side. "Say, you notice that I'm in an awful good mood today?"

I didn't notice, but that doesn't stop her.

"Good reason to be grinning ear to ear. Like I told you, Old Dryden will be hiding out in his cave 'til July fourth." This is the second time she's told me this. Why?

Evan shuts down the computer. "Gotta pick up my little sister at ballet. Catch you ladies later."

"Don't even try," Bertha mutters, tossing me some cloth napkins to fold for tomorrow's breakfast.

My napkins are a mess, not perky little dunce caps like Bertha's, because I'm busy thinking how this quasi relationship I have with a semisolid ghost isn't quite working for me.

Or is it? Suddenly he's there, just a shimmery flash of him in the dining room, hunched on the edge of the credenza, and then he's gone.

"Wait!" I whisper. "Don't go."

Bertha gives me a snarly look. "Whaddya want now?"

"No, not you," I murmur.

"You see anybody else?" She makes a big show of looking all around, under the stack of napkins, down the heat register, inside the silverware drawer.

"No, I don't see anybody else," I reply, but I wish I could corral that fleeting spirit and keep Nathaniel close long enough to ask him a few thousand questions. I will in the attic, if he shows and if he stays around long enough.

"See you later, Nathaniel," I whisper when Bertha retreats to the kitchen. I don't expect an answer.

"See-throughy images?" Nathaniel whispers, his tone slightly mocking.

I spin around and see him again, looking as handsome as ever, his dark eyes glinting mischievously. In the afternoon light, his uniform looks bluer than usual.

"You heard the whole conversation?" I snap, even though I'm thrilled to see him. "You've been spying on me!"

"Meet you in the attic," he replies, smiling. "Let's not wait until after the noon meal."

"Right now? I'll dash right upstairs."

"I'll get there before you," he teases.

"Well, yeah, since doors and walls are no obstacle." I slowly back away, then spin and run as fast as I can up three flights of stairs. Breathless, I push the ceiling door to the attic open, and Nathaniel's squatting there, ready to pull me up into the attic. He feels very much flesh-and-blood right now, but I gently push him away and lead him to the trunk.

He straddles it with me facing him, my back against a post and my legs crisscrossed.

"I'll tell you my story," he says.

9

I CAME UP in Punxsutawney," he begins.

"Punxsutawney!" I cut in, grinning. "You know what that city's famous for?"

"Coal mining, I would venture, and sand flies," Nathaniel responds.

"No! Punxsutawney Phil. Groundhog Day."

"Beg your pardon?"

"February second. The whole country waits for the famous groundhog, Punxsutawney Phil, to poke his head out of the ground. If he sees his shadow, we're in for six more weeks of winter." Which sounds appealing now, because it's sweltering up in the attic.

Nathaniel raises his eyebrows. "Well, I'll be. Punxsutawney Phil, eh? And if the famous groundhog doesn't see his shadow, we're in for roughly six more weeks of winter?" We both laugh at the absurdity of a rodent predicting the weather. Nathaniel's laugh is robust, full-bodied, and I've always been a sucker for great laughers.

"I suppose Punxsutawney Phil is long after my time, but Punx is where I grew up, in coal country. I was always playing alongside my friend Edison Larch. We weren't just friends, we were third cousins. Our fathers were partners in the Poseidon Coal Company, and I figured we'd be digging coal together until they planted us in Punxsutawney soil."

"That's amazing," I say truthfully. I have no friends that go back my whole life, not even Jocelyn. Living in one hotel after another doesn't breed lasting friendships. And then I feel a pang of sadness when I realize that Nathaniel was not laid to rest in his hometown.

A cloud passes over Nathaniel's face.

"What happened?" I ask.

"It was in eighteen and sixty. I was a young man by then. My father got wind that somebody'd struck oil up in Titusville, northeast of Punx. He sold our house and we were on our way before I could do a jig. Coal was good money, but people were saying it was just chicken feed compared to oil."

The words tumble out as though they've been banked for more than a century. I'm absorbing the details as fast as possible and somehow we've inched closer to each other and he reaches unconsciously for my hand.

"That last day before we moved, Edison asked me, 'You listening about the war and such?' Well, you couldn't miss listening. It was on everybody's lips. Edison thought those southern states had no right to pull out of the Union, and I told him what they had no right to do is keep slaves. One man owning another man? No, sir. Edison asked me if I was fixing to fight, since I was so worked up over the slavery question. Talk's one thing; shooting's another. I told him, not unless the fight comes right to my front door, and it didn't seem a whit likely it'd come up to Pennsylvania. But it came, didn't it? I joined up with the 93rd Pennsylvania regiment a couple weeks later."

His regiment — that gives me more to Google him with later. I have so many questions, including why he's buried in Evergreen instead of the National Soldier's Cemetery. But for now I wait and let Nathaniel continue.

"Last thing Edison said to me before my family left for Titusville was, 'So long, then, Nate. Come back to old Punx when you go broke. I'll still be here, if I don't get shot down in Mississippi or Georgia, one.'"

Nathaniel pauses just long enough for me to slip in a question: "Did you go back to see him again?"

"Did. But the Larches were gone. Things there soured like old milk."

"What happened to Edison?" I ask, trying to picture this old friend. Was he handsome like Nathaniel? For some reason I imagine him as smaller and slight.

Nathaniel peers over my shoulder, as if down through the tunnel of years. "Just after we moved to Titusville, Edison's family suffered a horrible tragedy. His father's custom was to inspect each of the mines every week."

I know nothing about coal mining, but Nathaniel explains that methane gas and coal dust can ignite, and the poor ventilation hundreds of feet into the Earth's core combine with the gases to create unspeakable disaster.

"That's why miners started sending a canary down there, to test the atmosphere, see if it was fit for humans to breathe. Mr. Larch, he was proud that not one trial canary had died in our mines in the past two years. So, that day he took up a lantern and went down into the pitch-black Earth's belly. He no sooner stepped off the elevator when he heard the roof rumbling. The wooden stakes supporting the roof starting buckling.

The rats scurried for an exit, but there wasn't one. The roof collapsed, most likely knocking the lantern out of Mr. Larch's hand, which set off an explosion with the trapped gasses. In my nightmares I see a raging river of fire. Only one man survived to tell the story. Not Edison Larch, Senior."

"How awful," I murmur.

Nathaniel rubs his face and stammers out his next words: "After that, my father got to be a mighty rich man. Edison's widowed mother, though, she was left poor as country peasants. I sent them some money, but Edison mailed it back to me with such a cruel letter. He let me know that he didn't need my charity, and that, in some strange way, he blamed me — my family — for their misfortune. The two were not connected, but in his mind, they were."

He sighs. I wonder why he's telling me all this. Do ghosts carry around guilt forever? If so, I don't want to die.

Nathaniel breathes heavily, and I sense that it's hard for him to suck in breath; this air is not his natural medium, especially in this sweltering attic. I wait.

"The Pierces and the Larches, we were linked in so many ways."

"Your fathers being in business and all," I say, to grease the flow of words.

He strokes his stubble, a *scritch* that's punctuated by a tree branch brushing the window. "More than our fathers," he begins. "More than Edison and me being friends and cousins. You see, I was set to marry his sister, Constance."

"Marry his *sister?*" I'm surprised to feel a jolt of jealousy. I have no reason to be upset about a girl who is now long dead. But I can't help it.

"You were engaged?" I demand.

"I was about to give Constance a ring, before I came to Gettysburg."

I pull my hand out of his, crushed to hear this news. Feebly, I say the only thing that's safe: "But you and Constance were cousins."

"Distant. It was common in my day for cousins to marry."

Then I blurt out what's *really* on my mind: "Did you love her, Nathaniel?"

"She was a handsome young woman, pleasant, familiar. We grew up together. It was always assumed we'd marry. But love her? No. She wasn't like you, free and vital."

I jump slightly at his words, new to my ears. Is he saying he didn't love her, but he loves *me?* My cheeks are burning. He hardly knows me. And I have no idea how I feel about him, deep down. I keep these thoughts to myself, but then I can't resist; I have to ask, trying to sound as calm as possible, "Whatever became of Constance Larch?"

"Word is she married a French blacksmith and moved to Louisiana. I suppose that put her on the opposite side of the War Between the States. We never met again, of course, because I was already dead."

"You've never seen her in the spirit realm?" I wonder if ghosts sort of drift toward each other like lazy clouds. Did Nathaniel float up to Constance, asking her help to solve his murder? I feel that stab of jealousy again.

Nathaniel seems surprised by the question. "Why, no. I've never had reason to reach her. She's gone; that's all there is to that. And you are here."

But where is *here* — on the *kalunga* line between the living and the dead? And how do we cross that line?

I take Nathaniel's hand again, feeling its misleading warmth. We look at each other, and I want to tell him to go on with his story — and I also want to lean in close to him — but then I hear my mother shouting, "Lori!" downstairs and I remember I was supposed to bring her the towels and help with the new guests. Before I can apologize to Nathaniel — or wonder if I can make up an excuse to Mom to stay in the attic — he's given me a quick smile and disappeared. Gone, again. For now.

10

I SIT BY the creek at nighttime, feeling more alone than I could ever imagine, listening to the screeching of a whippoorwill in a tree. Gertie is off with her new Chihuahua boyfriend, and Nathaniel seems to appear when it suits him. I sigh. Maybe I should just go back to the inn and Google Nathaniel, now that I know his regiment.

A light goes on in the lawn-mower shed up the hill, north of the house. Who'd be in there this late? Probably Dad scrounging around for some tools to fix the latest money-pit disaster.

Something about the garbage disposal backing up; he must be looking for the heavy-duty plunger.

I scoot up the bank, slip on my sandals, and start walking. The closer I get to the shed, the more uneasy I feel. Wish I'd brought Gertie with me, because someone's still in there.

"Dad?" As soon as the word's out of my mouth, the light flicks off. There's scurrying around inside; something crashes to the floor, followed by a gasp.

Is Dad hurt? I should go in and help, but my pulse is racing and thumping at the side of my head. Something tells me not to go in. It's like that scene in every scary movie when you want to scream at the girl, *Don't go in there! Don't open that door!*

Forget it. I unlatch the door. Inside it's totally dark. As my eyes adjust, I make out the lawn mower and hoes and shovels standing like silent skeletons. I have a vision of a rake coming to life, chasing me with its vicious claws. Things like this *never* used to creep into my head. But now that I'm certain ghosts are real, I'm wondering if there's something sinister about Coolspring Inn, maybe even a person, or an entity of some sort that doesn't want me here.

Something that seemed frozen in place moves! Just enough for me to register that it's alive. I'm pumped with adrenaline. I take baby steps back toward the door. Whoever or whatever is hiding in the corner can't see me any better than I can see it. Suddenly the figure sinks to the floor, crouching behind something — maybe a gas drum or a gunnysack of fertilizer. Nothing's clear except shape and shadow. The figure's crab-walking across the floor. I stare in fascination, too paralyzed to run. But then, running would make me too obvious a target. Flowerpots go flying and shattering in its wake as the figure darts toward the back of the shed. The top half of the split door opens. Moonlight floods the shed as the intruder catapults over the bottom half of the door. From the back, it could be anybody, but at least I know it's not an any*thing.*

Who might have been snooping around in the shed? Could it have been Nathaniel? But why would he run away from me? I hope it's not some other ghost. One's all I can handle.

I can't remember if the shed is usually locked, but even if it wasn't locked, somebody crept in who shouldn't have; somebody who didn't want to get caught. *Think, Lori!* The figure could have been male or female. Too thin to be Bertha. Too upright to be Old Dryden. Had to be somebody pretty limber to leap over the half door. Maybe it was Evan Maxwell? But why would he have to sneak in and out under cover of darkness, when he's got access to the shed all the time? Or was it Dad? Why would he hide and crawl across the floor? Maybe he thought he was the one who belonged in the shed, but *I* was some dangerous intruder that he needed to escape from. But no, it's not Dad's style to slink away in fear. He's more likely to be the guy awakened by a suspicious sound in the middle of the night who goes downstairs to confront the intruder with a Pennsylvania-ash baseball bat. And he must have heard me yell, "Dad!"

Nothing makes sense.

Outside the shed, I listen in the steamy night for movement, footsteps, crunched gravel. It's quiet as a cavern; even the whippoorwill had the good sense to shut up. The moon slides in and out of sight, obscured by tall pines. I turn and hurry toward the house, try the front door.

No! Mom locks it at ten o'clock, and I forgot my key. I lean on the bell until Mom opens the little peephole in the red door.

"Oh, Lori, it's you, in one piece. My goodness, I thought it was a dire emergency." She opens the door and drags me inside, sighing in relief.

In the quiet of my tower room, my body stops ticking like a demented clock. I manage to change into my pj's and crawl under the covers. The reassuring drone of Amelia Wilhoit's printer in the room under me lulls me to sleep.

The next morning I wake refreshed; no spooky dreams or shimmery night visitors. Last night's incident in the shed seems innocent in the sunlight.

But then, as I'm getting dressed, I notice a small, folded-up note has been slipped under my door. Feeling a prickle of fear, I pick up the note and unfold it cautiously. Printed in big block letters on Coolspring Inn stationery are the words, *FRET NOT — OTHERS SEE THEM, TOO.* No signature.

Who's *them*? Shadowy figures running out of the shed in the middle of the night? Or ghosts? Could it be that somebody else in the house sees spirits? I know Charlotte does, but she wouldn't have sent me a note — we'd talked about it already. What's the point of the note? To reassure me that I'm not nuts? Or is it some sort of warning?

I'm mulling all these questions over in my mind as I finish dressing and hurry downstairs to help Hannah with breakfast. Is *she* the one who wrote the note? I check her out for a conspiratorial glance — *ha-ha, we're in this weird space together, kid, both of us hanging on the* kalunga *line.*

But Hannah is as no-nonsense as always as she bustles around the kitchen. On the counter there's a mountain of gaping orange halves. Hannah says, "Toss those rinds in the compost heap, dearie. The worms adore oranges. I wouldn't dare put all that stuff down the disposal, the way it's been acting up. Your poor father had to get down into the throat of the pipe again."

I nod, feeling relieved as I spot the industrial-strength yellow stick plunger in the corner. So *it* was probably Dad in the shed last night, getting the plunger, and he thought I was an intruder. But something still doesn't sit right with me.

After breakfast, I e-mail Randy.

> **LoriC@squareone.com**
> Up for a Skype chat, Randy?

> **RWChase@Tennyson.edu**
> [auto-response] Hey, friends, I'm out in
> the villages upriver. Won't return to
> civilization, e.g., Internet, until July 4.
> Happy Independence Day, all you
> Americans. Independence Day 'round
> here is March 6. Get back to you ASAP.

Deflated, I try Jocelyn. Wish I could text her. She's not great about responding to my e-mails. I guess the horsey girls don't give her much free time, or there aren't good hot spots at the camp. Too bad, because everything around here is getting hotter by the minute.

LoriC@squareone.com

Hey, Jos. What would you think if you were in a pitch-dark garden shed & heard someone else in there, but you couldn't see him, & then he dropped to the floor & took a flying leap over the split door to escape you? Make that *me*. Crazy things are happening here, & I'm, oh, a tad confused. Help!

I realize it sounds hysterical and melodramatic, so I delete the whole message and slip into my running shorts, T-shirt, and sneakers. I sprint downstairs with one of my softballs. It feels good to toss it hand to hand while I pass by Gertie. She's been sniffing around for Brownie, who's out doing the Gettysburg tourist thing with her owners.

"Let's go outside, Gertie Girl." That pacifies her, and she's down the stairs in a flash, nosing at the back door. Outside, a rabbit crosses her path, and she barks madly and chases the terrorized creature.

Evan Maxwell comes running around the house, clutching garden shears. "What's happening here?" he asks breathlessly. "I heard Gertie going nuts."

"She's so brave, chasing a rabbit one-tenth her size. Hey, I'm glad you're here."

"You are?" He stands up taller and sweeps a sweaty lock of hair off his forehead. "Happy to see me — that's the best news of the day, compared to the other news, from Princeton. A thick envelope from a university is great. This was a thin envelope."

"I'm sorry, Evan. Was Princeton your first choice?"

"Third. I'm holding out for Stanford. I was wait-listed there, too."

A tiny glimmer of disappointment surprises me: He'll be off to college in the fall. But then I think, *Why should I care? We're not really friends.* "Can we talk about something that's bugging me?" I ask him.

Evan drops the clippers, grabs the softball out of my hand, and backs away. "Here, catch." He hurls the ball in a wobbly arc toward me. I get under it easily and pitch it back.

"Hey, good arm," he says, fumbling the ball. Gertie's running from me to him, but is smart enough to realize it's our game, not hers. "So, what's on your mind, Lori?"

"It's about the lawn-mower shed."

He moves in closer and flings the ball in my general direction, which is to say, at a puddle by a rosebush. He'd *never* have made the mixed league in Philly.

"Yeah, I know. Some animal got in there and burrowed into a corner when the door was open yesterday. Poor critter must have panicked when he couldn't get out. *Ooof!*" The ball thuds into his belly, and he staggers back. "Game over. So, I figure when dinnertime came, the animal pecked open the bag of bedding soil looking for munchies. Dirt and broken pots are all over the floor, and some clippers and trowels were knocked off the hooks. It's a mess. I better clean it up before Old Dryden resurfaces."

"What kind of animal?" I ask.

"Squirrel? Possum, maybe? This used to be their hangout before we civilized it."

I accept the muddy ball back from Evan, digging my fingers into its sides. "I think it was a human animal, Evan."

Evan furrows his brow. "Nah. An actual human wouldn't have any reason to rip open a sack of soil."

"Unless he was looking for something."

"In a pile of dirt? Come on."

"I saw someone run out the back door of the shed," I tell him quietly. "Someone who didn't want to get caught in there."

"Hmm. I'll check it out later today," Evan tells me, and I

feel slightly better. "Got to pick up my uniform at the cleaners now," he adds, checking his watch. "Score a few canisters of fake blood, a musket, some ammo. I'm dying at one forty-six tomorrow. Come watch."

Right. The reenactment of the Battle. "I don't think so," I tell him. "I don't have the stomach for it."

"Hey, it's human epic to the max. Blood and guts, pain and agony, good guys and bad guys. It's classic, like *The Godfather* or *The Hunger Games* on a beautiful summer afternoon. People eat it up."

"Maybe," I offer dubiously, backing up toward the house.

"Yeah, I know what you mean," he says quietly, all the bravado leaked away. "It's Gettysburg in July."

11

LATER THAT EVENING, long after dinner, I flop down on my bed and open my laptop to finally Google Nathaniel and his regiment. But then suddenly, something feels off-kilter. My bedroom door slams, although there's no breeze. The air has that leaden feeling, heavier than mere heat and humidity.

"You're here, aren't you?" I whisper, and my heart leaps with joy.

A disembodied voice says, "We haven't much time, Lorelei, and there's still so much to tell you."

"I know, Nathaniel," I say, glancing around and seeing no one else in my room. Then my pleasure morphs into indignation. "But where are you? You can't just keep showing up and disappearing without warning. Or talking to me when I can't see you! Let's set some ground rules. Because right now you have all the advantages. Relationships in my world are fifty-fifty."

Are we in a relationship? I wonder. *Is that even possible?*

The warm, familiar voice replies from seemingly nowhere. "I'm at a great *dis*advantage, Lorelei, with words in your world. But I can guess the meaning of fifty-fifty."

"That's a start. Okay, Number One: You can't hover around me and listen in on my conversations without my knowledge."

"I try not to, I do, but it's so much harder to resist than to give in to the impulse."

I nod. "Like trying to give up French fries." I realize he doesn't *get* French fries. Oh, well. "Rule Number Two: Please show yourself when you talk. Otherwise I feel silly just spitting words out in your general direction. I look like a crazy person."

"Aye, General." He shimmers into visibility, perched on my desk, and I'm struck again by how dashing and melancholy and strong he looks — for a dead person. There's a scent about him that's like cinnamon or ginger. I want to hurry over to him, to be close to him, but I try to stand my ground.

"Rule Number Three —"

"You're quite the bossy girl, aren't you?"

"Of course. I'm a Scorpio!"

"You don't look a bit like a scorpion, for which I'm immensely grateful." I want to laugh, figuring it's not worth explaining astrology to him. Then he holds out his foot toward me, the one bound in cloth and scraps of leather. "That's how I lost my boot, when a scorpion took up lodging in it. I saw him down in the dark of the toe and tossed the boot as far as I could. It landed in a campfire. Both the boot and the scorpion, fried crisp. The scorpion was more tasty than the boot."

"Why, Nathaniel Pierce, you have a sense of humor."

He smiles shyly. "Have we finished with the rules?"

"One more. I'll meet you anywhere but here in my room or the bathroom." Although part of me loves having Nathaniel in my room, another part of me feels like it's too big of a step, too quickly. I want to be able to move freely about my room without worrying about my privacy or the peering eyes of a handsome ghost.

"The bathroom?" Nathaniel asks. His quizzical look reminds me that he comes from a time before indoor plumbing.

"The water closet, the loo?" I offer, thinking, for some reason, of British slang. "The . . . facilities?"

"Ah, the privy."

"Yes! As in *private*."

"I understand," he says, all proper and gentlemanly.

"Okay. Then I'd say we're done with rules for now." I stand and walk over to him. We are close enough that our elbows collide. I'm glad that I showered after tossing around the softball outside, and that I changed into a sleeveless yellow sundress to feel cooler. Nathaniel puts his firm hands on my shoulders and draws me closer. He's solid now, as real as I am, but no body heat radiates from him, and even up against his chest I feel no heartbeat.

I have so much to learn about ghosts.

"A question for you," I whisper to him, grateful that most of the guests and my parents are sleeping and can't hear me conversing in the night. "You weren't in the shed last night, were you? I saw — something."

Concern flashes across Nathaniel's face but he shakes his head. "No. I was in the cemetery, by my grave, but thinking of you. Why?"

I don't want to get into the mystery with him now. I notice him glance from me to the laptop on my bed.

"You opened your talking machine," he says. "May I see how it operates?"

Why not? I grab my laptop and drop to the floor while he

sits behind me on my bed. I click a few keys and feel him watching me with avid curiosity.

I enter *Nathaniel Pierce 93rd regiment Gettysburg* into the Search bar.

"You can put my name into this machine?" Nathaniel asks with incredulity.

"You can't imagine what this machine can do," I tell him.

The search results pop up, and I click on the first article. I begin reading, instinctively hunching over so that Nathaniel can't see what I see. I'm not sure why I want this privacy — maybe it's the same reason I felt indignant when he just showed up in my room.

July 3, 1863 — Private Nathaniel Pierce, of Titusville, Pennsylvania, a member of the 93rd Pennsylvania Volunteers, succumbed to a bullet wound to the back. There is reason to believe that Pierce was guilty of treason . . .

My heart stops. *What?* I keep reading.

. . . and was executed, according to the unofficial military custom of the time. Because the evidence

*of the treason is inconclusive, Pierce was not
buried in the Pennsylvania section of the National
Military Cemetery at Gettysburg. It is unknown
where his remains lie.*

I snap around to face him, my cheeks burning.

"You're a *traitor?*" I demand. "After all your high-minded ideas about the evils of slavery, you betrayed the Union?"

Nathaniel's eyes widen. "Is that what you think?"

"It's not about what I think. It's about what I'm reading right now." I slam the laptop shut, feeling ready to crumble into a heap. "And you weren't murdered — it says right here you were executed."

This isn't possible. This can't be the Nathaniel I've come to know. He couldn't have sabotaged the northern war effort, or spied on the Union and passed strategic information to the Confederate army. I can't believe this.

But it's true he didn't have an honorable burial in the sol-dier's cemetery. My stomach tightens. What do I actually know about this young man from the past, except for his story about his friend Edison, and Nathaniel's father's fortune in oil?

"What do you want me to tell you?" he asks wearily.

"The truth. Simple enough."

"The truth is slippery."

I shiver. What if it *is* true, that he is guilty of treason? How could he pass himself off as a respectable soldier and the victim of a murderer? Setting me up. Making me care for him deep in my soul. Blood's pumping through my head. I jump to my feet and stomp around my room, hands on hips. He must be able to see the pulse throbbing at my temples. How could he deceive me this way?

"Come sit down, please." He reaches for my hand. I resist for a moment. There's a ropy scar like a solid worm on his palm, something I haven't noticed before. It couldn't be a new wound, could it? My eyebrows rise in question. But still, I take his hand and we slide down to the floor together. We sit with our backs against the bed.

Nathaniel releases my hand and shows me his scar again. "Burned by a musket. Those guns got very hot as the battle raged one hour after the next and those minié balls were flying. Once that first burn blistered, I kept a rag in my haversack so I didn't fry any more flesh."

So much to absorb — musket, haversack, minié. I realize he's watching me, still holding out his hand. For one crazy moment it feels like a marriage proposal, with him gazing long-ingly into my eyes. It's not. I blink first.

"Time will take me away from you in three days," he says, "and the pain'll be as sharp as my bayonet wound. If I leave you and there are no answers, I'll continue in torment, Lorelei."

"Oh, really? What about my torment, not knowing if you were a traitor?"

"There's so much more to tell," he begins, his resonant voice low and distant.

"Just explain this," I say, my anger somewhat tempered but my suspicion still raging. "If it says here you were shot for treason, then you weren't murdered."

"But I was," Nathaniel protests. "I believe to this day that my death was explained away as my being shot for treason, when in truth that wasn't what happened at all."

"So tell me what happened." I've got my legs hunched up. Pressing my chin into my knees keeps my mouth shut, so this has always been my best listening posture.

"When I joined up with the 93rd Regiment early in 1863, I wondered if my friend Edison was still alive and fighting this war. He would have gone for cavalry, felt more at home on horseback than on his own feet. I searched for him here in Gettysburg, but there were thousands of soldiers on both sides — infantry, cavalry, artillery, fife-and-drummers, wheelwrights, blacksmiths, medics. I couldn't find him.

"After the first hot night of battle, I was so stirred up that I couldn't sleep. What kept haunting me was that I might've killed a man. Maybe more. I'd just kept reloading my musket as fast as possible and firing it across the stretch between us and them. Men toppled in the field; horses, too. Do you know how awful the stench of horse flesh is decaying in the July sun?"

I can't begin to imagine — it's as alien to me as my laptop is to Nathaniel. Now Nathaniel's breath comes in shallow gasps. He's far away from me, steeped in the visions and smells, and then he wrenches himself back, squeezing my hand. Pleasure flutters up my arm despite all the horror he's lugged from his past into the present.

"So, I sat on a boulder that had served as a barricade earlier in the day. Along came a man lighting up a Bull Durham. Said, 'Evening, soldier,' and we exchanged pleasantries. He was a surgeon; I don't recall his name. Told me he'd met someone who was looking for a Nathaniel Pierce, or might have been Nathan Price, and he couldn't recall the other soldier's name, either."

"Not too good with details, was he?" I mutter. "Great for a doctor. I hope he didn't mix up lungs and kidneys. You think he was talking about Edison?"

"Don't know. He told me he'd heard how desperate the Union was for surgeons, so he'd come up from Baltimore to volunteer. The year before he'd been attending President Lincoln's family. I suspected he wasn't telling the truth. We all embellished memories, promoting plain girlfriends to beauties and simple meals to feasts, to get us through the horrors of the war.

"So, the doctor talked about his White House days, how Mr. Lincoln was depressed by the war and the tragedy in his family. He'd already lost one son, Edward, and now another son, William, lay on his deathbed, but eleven years old. I can tell you, I was in no mood for a heartbreaking story after all I'd seen in a day of battle, but the doctor's wheels were greased, and there was no stopping him. While William raged with fever, Doc told me, a ring on his bloated thumb cut into his flesh. Doc soaped the finger and massaged the ring off. Minutes later, William Lincoln stopped breathing."

My legs shoot out from under my chin as my heart swells with grief. "Oh, poor President Lincoln. How could they bear losing two sons?"

"You're a tender thing, you are." Nathaniel pulls me close. Our shoulders are pressed together. "The surgeon said there was no consoling them. Mrs. Lincoln wept and keened for hours, and the president himself shed tears. After they said their final farewells, Doc found the ring in the folds of the sheets. He handed it to Mrs. Lincoln, but she was wild and exhausted with grief, and reared back as though he were offering her a live serpent."

"So, what finally happened to the ring?" I ask, locked securely in Nathaniel's wingspan, though the rough wool of his uniform scratches my bare arm.

"The doctor kept it, later put it on the thumb of his own grandson. But then, that night when we spoke, he pulled a green pouch out of his pocket and removed the ring from it. He held it up, gold and glinting in the moonlight. Said, 'I took back Mr. Lincoln's ring when it grew too tight for my boy's finger, and it's been my lucky charm ever since. Pray to God it'll see me through this bloody war.'"

It all feels mysterious and thrilling, this strange, spooky connection to Abraham Lincoln himself. But . . .

"What does this have to do with your murder?" I ask Nathaniel. "And the treason charge?"

His dark eyes are wide and solemn. "If you are willing to stay awake and hear it, I will explain everything."

"I'm willing," I say.

12

WE HUDDLE TOGETHER on the floor in my room. It's
past midnight, same as the night Nathaniel is now telling me
about, back in Gettysburg all those years ago.

"It was black as pitch, July second. You'd think the moon
was ashamed to cast her countenance upon the bodies strewn
in the Wheatfield. Finally, the guns were quiet for the night. I
was long past limp with exhaustion and sorrow after two days
of battle, but General Sickles ordered all the able-bodied men
to bring in the dead. My friend Wince Carmody and I thanked

the good Lord that somebody else was on the burial detail, already digging shallow graves."

My ears perk up. "Carmody? This inn is the Vienna Carmody House."

Nathaniel nods. "Called after his wife. He built the house for her a dozen years after the war."

I file this info away and wring my hands, urging him to get on with the story.

"So that night, I collapsed right where I landed, preferring to sleep in the dirt rather than struggling to my tent. Seemed like only a minute later when someone called my name. One of the drummer boys said, 'Private Pierce, sir? I hate to bother you, sleeping like you was, but there's another one out there.'"

My heart jumps. "Another what?" I ask, picturing a field of bodies and dead horses and blood-soaked ground.

Nathaniel squeezes my hand, which makes my heart jump again, but also soothes me. He goes on.

"The boy said, 'A live one, sir. Don't know if he's one of ours, sir. Too dark to tell.' He stood by, with a drum slung across his chest as a futile deflector of bullets, waiting until I could drag myself up. We stepped around Confederate bodies. Facedown in the stiff grass lay a soldier moaning, calling for his mother. I turned him over and saw he was no older than the drummer boy, maybe fourteen, and he was a Reb. Entrails spilled out of the jagged hole in the boy's gut. His eyes were glazed over, but when my face came close, they filled with fear.

"I told him, 'I'll not hurt you, little brother. We'll carry you to a hospital and see what the medics can do for you.' He cried out as we hoisted his shattered body onto the stretcher and carried him to the hospital, the one that stood up the hill there before the old house burned down."

I chew the inside of my cheek, a stress habit. "Tell me they saved that poor kid."

Nathaniel raises and drops his shoulders in a sigh of grief. "The docs had been working day and night. So many wounded all over the hospital. Most of the docs went home to rest a few hours before the battle would take up again in the morning. The only one on duty was that doctor I'd met earlier, and he was nearly sleeping on his feet."

"The guy with Lincoln's ring, right?"

Nathaniel nods again and shifts beside me. It's amazing how comfortable I feel by his side, our hands interlocked as he talks. I've never felt this sort of ease touching a boy before.

"So would a Union doctor treat an enemy soldier?" I ask, trying to sort things out. "Is *that* treason?"

"It didn't matter to the medics, Yank or Reb; it was a human life. The doctor knelt beside the Reb, shaking his head. Even if the boy survived the gunshot wound, the pain would still be unbearable, and he'd soon die of infection; half his insides were out. But the doctor did what he could for the boy. Then in came Henry Baldwin, a soldier in my infantry. He had his wounded brother slung over his shoulder. When Henry saw that the patient I'd brought in was a Confederate, he flew into a rage, grabbed the doctor by his shirt, and tried to pull him away from the boy. The doctor wrenched himself loose and continued to treat the boy while Henry Baldwin's brother bled out. Died."

My heart sinks. "That's terrible," I whisper, even though I know Nathaniel witnessed so many other deaths. I can't fathom it.

Nathaniel shakes his head; his long hair tickles my neck. "Henry went berserk and started throwing wild punches. Landed one on the side of the doctor's head. I wrestled Henry to the ground. The drummer boy sat on him to keep him still 'til he simmered down. And then Baldwin said, 'What you done, Pierce, it's worse'n being a Rebel; it's treason, letting the enemy get took care of before one of our own. Best watch your back. You know what comes to traitors, don'tcha?'"

"What comes to traitors?" I ask, although I've just read it online, but I need to hear it from Nathaniel's mouth.

Nathaniel gets up and circles the room. I watch him, missing his presence beside me. Then he sits down on the bed behind me, resting his hands on my shoulders. They're light and heavy at the same time. I lay my cheek on his hand.

"The punishment for treason is death," he says softly. "Killing a traitor's an honorable deed. Any soldier can do it, just shoot you dead."

I swerve around to face Nathaniel, feeling my eyes widen. "Then Henry Baldwin was the one who killed you! Not murder. It was execution. But you weren't committing treason, Nathaniel. You were saving a life, not betraying your country." I'm flooded with relief to know this about him.

Nathaniel shakes his head again.

"Henry Baldwin didn't kill me that night, and I'm not sure if he was the one who eventually shot me dead. I lived to see another day of battle. By then, we were nearly out of ammunition. Enemy was, too. We were sent into hand-to-hand combat, so close I could see the color of the enemies' eyes. We'd been fighting dawn to dusk, and Meade's army was nearing defeat. The Rebs were after Culp's Hill, which we were doing our best to hold on to. The guns quieted for two minutes, and some of the men made a run for it to find a safer position. That was when I thought I saw Edison Larch running off a ways."

I give a start. "Edison? Your childhood friend?"

"Yes, but I couldn't be sure," Nathaniel says. "I was exhausted. I lost sight of him, and then the bullets started flying again, and that was the last of it. Could've been; could've *not* been." Nathaniel takes a deep breath. "But that distraction cost me. I was stabbed in the shoulder, and overcome by a terrible pain."

"Oh no." I lean in closer, drenched in misery for him. My feelings are all twisted into knots of belief and doubt. I wonder if this cascade of feelings is normal for . . . love.

Nathaniel goes on. "I stumbled into my tent, joining a dozen other battle-dazed men. I collapsed on my cot, pressing a bloody rag to my shoulder and clenching my teeth to steel myself against the pain."

My hand flies to my own shoulder, burning as if I were feeling Nathaniel's searing pain myself.

"As I fell onto the cot, I noticed a small green pouch in the corner, and I recognized it — it belonged to the doctor. My wound was making me delirious but I remember reaching inside and finding the ring. President Lincoln's ring. The doctor's lucky charm. In my haze, I thought that I should keep it for him. He must have dropped it after tending to another wounded soldier."

I nod, trying to imagine the scene in the tent. The chaos and confusion. Nathaniel continues.

"My good friend Wince Carmody, he'd spent a month studying surgery before the war, so he knew what he was doing."

"A month, and he was a surgeon? It takes eight years now
to learn that stuff."

"How much could there be to learn?" he asks incredulously.
"Wince knew what to do. He cut the torn jacket away from my
shoulder, cleaned the wound with a sliver of soap from his haversack, and bound the shoulder in a figure eight, under and over
my arm. Used a hank of cloth torn from his own sheet as a
bandage. Then he boiled a healing tea — lavender and mint I
think it was — to soothe me to sleep. I knew the pain would
surge back to me with the coming dawn.

"I was in twilight, not sure if I was awake or asleep, when
Henry Baldwin burst into our tent. The doctor was right behind
him, wildly shouting about how one of us, Baldwin or I, stole
something of value from him. I could barely keep my eyes open,
and couldn't have lifted my head, but Wince got up to settle
the argument. The doc was in a frenzy of rage, demanding to
know which one of us was the thief. Baldwin shouted at the doctor, 'You're one to talk, you murderer, you. You let my brother
Jimbo bleed to death right there in front of you while you fussed
over a enemy soldier which was drug in by Pierce, over there,
fakin' injury.'

"Baldwin pointed to me, called me a cowardly traitor for

letting his brother die. He squatted beside my cot, tried to rough me up a little, and all I could do was grunt with the pain, until the doctor put a stop to it by yanking Baldwin up. I sank back, the pain scorching me something fierce. Doc was glaring at me and hissing, 'You know what was stolen, what I treasured above all else, Pierce.'"

I sit up straight. "The ring! Abraham Lincoln's ring! The one you found on the cot!"

"Yes, Lorelei, but I wasn't putting two and two together then, hanging on the edge of life like I was. In that moment, I had completely forgotten I had the ring on me. By then, all the men in the tent were awake, some hurting from wounds, and all hollering for quiet, and Wince asked what it was the doctor was missing. He answered, 'A small thing wrapped up tight in a green bag. I'd rather not say what; it's personal.' He said Baldwin probably took it out of his pocket and Baldwin shouted, 'You accusin' me, a man what just lost his one and only brother? You are a cold fish, Doc, cold as an arctic blast.'"

Nathaniel's breath comes in shallow gasps. He's far away from me, steeped in the visions and smells, and then he wrenches himself back, squeezing my hand.

"So, the doctor turned hateful eyes on me, said I must have reached into his pocket while the fight with Baldwin was swinging left and right."

"But you were practically dead," I remind Nathaniel.

"I was, but Doc was a madman that night, not thinking straight because he hadn't slept in three nights. Well, then, Wince pushed Baldwin out of our tent and asked, could the doctor have just dropped the treasure. Doc shook his head, telling us it was an amulet that had kept him alive even when he was out there on the battlefield bringing in the wounded while bullets were flying. Gentling down a little, he brushed his ashen face with dry-papery hands. Even with one eye open, I could see blood embedded under his fingernails. Then, like a man defeated, he staggered out of the tent.

"So, after things calmed down, I tried to sleep. My pulse was racing and I knew I was in bad shape, losing so much blood. I put my hand to my heart to try to slow its drumming and tapped something in my pocket. With my one good hand, I slid the small green bag out of the pocket."

"The doctor's ring," I say.

Nathaniel nods. "I promised myself that I'd return it to the doctor, soon as I had the strength to get up on my feet. I sure didn't want to carry the guilt to the grave, just in case I didn't make it through the night."

"Tell me you did *not* steal the ring from the doctor."

"I did not. At least, I think I didn't."

"Wouldn't you know? Anyway, what reason on earth would

you have to steal it?" I ask indignantly, feeling doubt creeping back into my bones.

"Reason, Lorelei? Wasn't a lot of it during those three days of battle. You have to understand the stresses and perplexity, the pain, the noise, the putrid stench of rotting flesh, the blood-slippery ground, the exhaustion. All that'll drive a man to insanity, believe me. Believe me," he says again.

I nod. I do.

"I managed to wake Wince and he promised to take care of the ring, to bring it to the doctor in the morning. He sat me up then to spoon a little tea in my mouth. And that's —" He shakes his head. "That is the last real memory I have of that night. There was something of a scuffle in the tent, and then a loud shot. I felt a pain in my back that was at once sharper and duller than the pain in my shoulder. I don't think I'd even realized I'd been shot. The next thing I knew, I was floating up and seeing my dead body, from a great distance. But I couldn't see anything else around me. It was all black and fuzzy. I don't know who killed me, or why."

There's a long silence. Tears fill my throat, and I'm about to ask him if he has any suspects. But then I hear thundering footsteps that stop at my door, and a furious knock.

"Mrs. Chase! Mrs. Chase! HELP!"

13

I RECOGNIZE THE young voices, and I leap to my feet. "It's the McLean boys. You'd better go, Nathaniel."

He nods, and the air around me changes so that I know he's gone just as the door bursts open and the boys, plus Brownie the dog, trot right into my room.

"I'm not a missus anybody," I tell them, annoyed at being interrupted. My thoughts are still on Nathaniel and the horrible story he told me. "My name's Lori. Why did you rampage in here like the house was going up in smoke?"

Then I notice that Max is all blubbery with tears, and I feel bad. Jake, the older boy, can barely get his words out.

"We — we heard somebody downstairs who wasn't s'posed to be."

"I'm sure it's just one of our guests having a restless night, pacing around the parlor," I tell them, but I can't help but feel a twinge of fear. Is Nathaniel still here somewhere, listening? If I knew he was close by, I'd feel safer.

Jake shakes his head wildly. "Me and Max were sleeping next to an open window, and we heard an awful scream. Honest. Cross my heart and hope to die."

"Please don't die on my watch," I say.

Jake continues in a panic. "So me and Max went exploring and we saw a guy going down to the basement."

The night is hot and still; not a breath of wind, but I feel chilled to the bone. I try to remain calm, though. I tell them, "It's an old house. The floors creak, wind wails through the walls. There are shadows in strange places." *Oh, and there's a ghost here, too.* "Besides," I add, "why didn't you tell your parents what you saw?"

Max is still sniffling. Jake replies, "There'd be no point in trying to wake them. Daddy could sleep through a bomb blast," Jake says. "Mama, too."

I heave a sigh. The skeptical side of me is certain they've been imagining things, but I can't help thinking of that figure in the shed. Even though I'm scared, I grab my flashlight. I try to be brave, like Nathaniel was as a soldier. I usher the boys and Brownie out of my room.

"Okay, let's go see," I tell them. "I'll show you there's nobody there."

The wide beam of the flashlight livens every corner on the second floor, where all the bedroom doors are closed. No screams. Something Bertha said flashes through my mind: People staying in this house have reported hearing the screams of wounded soldiers, or at least of their spirits that linger in agonized eternity.

We creep down another flight of stairs, and I flip all the switches to flood the first floor with light. Mom and Dad's door is closed. All the public rooms are empty, and Gertie's deep into dreamland in her doggy bed on the screened porch. I turn my flashlight toward the boys and Brownie, who tries to leap out of Jake's arms to cuddle with Gertie.

The light at the top of the steep, narrow basement stairs is just a bare bulb, very dim, but I bathe the steps ahead of us with my high-beam flashlight. My knees are knocking. I don't want the boys to see that my hands are shaking, so I steady the flashlight and we start down the creaky stairs. Everything smells sour, like laundry left overnight in the washer.

The original kitchen was in the basement, and there's a leftover coal-burning stove shoved into a corner, tilting on three legs. Its black ventilation chute reaches up and stops just short of the ceiling, which is crisscrossed with exposed pipes coated with white plaster. Water rushes through the pipes; maybe someone flushed a toilet upstairs. Good. At least someone else is awake in the house to hear us if we scream.

There's not much stored in the basement except folding chairs and a rolled-up carpet and some paint drums. Otherwise, the room is empty. Relief rushes through me.

"See? All clear. Nobody down here," I whisper. "Let's all go up to bed."

Jake opens the oven door and sticks his head into the gaping black. "Nobody in there," he announces. Then Max kicks over a plastic crate, and behind it is a tiny skeleton of a squirrel or raccoon.

"Cool!"Jake cries.

"Don't touch it, guys." Didn't I read somewhere that you can get rabies from animal carcasses? These bones are so dry, though, that they'd turn to powder with the slightest pressure.

Jake points to a door on the west wall. "Where's that go?"

"Water heater, furnace, that stuff. Back to bed."

"I hear something in there, don't you?" Jake tiptoes over to the door. Brownie's *yip-yapping* in his staccato bark that wouldn't scare anything mightier than a gnat. When Jake reaches for the doorknob, it rattles loose and comes off in his hand. "Yipes!" He drops it like it's steaming.

"Shh. You too, Brownie." Now I also hear something on the other side of the door. "Get behind me, boys." My heart is racing. I wriggle my finger in the doorknob hole to work the latch; the door swings open. We all three jump back in shock, the boys clinging to my skirt.

Old Dryden's in there on the floor, his butt sticking out from under a table! He turns his head toward us, eyes wild with fear — or is it fury?

Brownie's a wreck, running around in circles while Max tries to shush him.

"What are you doing?" I ask Old Dryden. He stands and smoothes down the Hawaiian shirt that's riding up over his bowling-ball belly. The boys peek around me, still glued to my waist, and Jake asks boldly, "Were you the one doing all that screaming bloody murder?"

Old Dryden snarls. "Never made a peep 'til you come along."

"But we heard you," Max cries, trying to hold a struggling Brownie.

"Raging spirits," Old Dryden says. "Left over from the hospital days." His face cruelly twists. "Doctor only needed twelve minutes to cut off a whole leg. Arm, less than that."

I'm no longer frightened, just annoyed. "You are totally scaring the boys, Mr. Dryden. Why are you still here at this hour?"

He doesn't answer me.

"Jake and Max, go on upstairs, quick. Get in your room and lock the door." I hear their footsteps scamper across the kitchen floor above me. I'm alone with Old Dryden, which is not smart. I march him toward the stairs with the flashlight thrust into his back, kidney level. Of course, he could kill me just by backing up and butting me down the stairs, but he's clutching the banister and breathing heavily, one slow step at a time, probably concentrating on just staying alive 'til the top. The man needs a fitness program.

At the garden door, I watch him with narrowed eyes as he staggers out into the night. Then I throw the bolt so he can't get back in.

But how did he get in in the first place?

Back in my own room upstairs, I tumble into my bed fully clothed. This is getting to be a bad habit.

As I'm trying to set my heart to normal speed, I wonder about Old Dryden. He's supposed to be sleeping, hibernating, like Bertha said, until July fourth. In his own house. What's he doing prowling around in our basement, and if he had a legitimate reason to be there, why was he hiding? Too many bizarre things going on here. I need a reasonable person to help me sort all this out. I slide my laptop out from under the bed, open Skype, and click on Randy's name.

It's early morning in Ghana. He doesn't pick up. I hit the phone icon again, listen to the chirpy ring, get the message *Call Ended.* Then I remember he said he'd be out in some village visiting the sacred crocodiles or hippos. Out there on the savanna, the only electricity is from a generator, probably hand-cranked, for a six-bed hospital in a Quonset hut. Jocelyn is almost just as hard to reach. But I've got to get some answers somewhere. I wish Nathaniel were here now, but I still don't know how to *call* him. And I've stupidly told him not to hover around or pop up unexpectedly.

Evan. I don't have his cell number, can't text him, and certainly can't call his house phone in the middle of the night. But I know his e-mail, so I send him a quick message. No answer. I decide not to stay up waiting, so I close my "talking machine," as Nathaniel calls it, and drift into an uneasy sleep.

14

IT'S THE FIRST day of the Battle reenactment, which means in two days Nathaniel will be gone. I feel a little flutter of panic about having only two more days to possibly help him, and also about him leaving so soon. But I push it aside.

I come downstairs in shorts and a tank top, feeling groggy. The McLean boys are snarfing down pancakes drowned in blackberry syrup. "Keep your purple tongues in your mouths, boys," Mrs. McLean scolds as she pops a bite of Canadian bacon into the gaping mouth of Brownie, hiding in her beach bag.

I give the boys the lip-tapping *shoosh* signal and whisper, "It's our secret, got it?" Jake nods. Max looks like I'd eat him alive if he breathed a word about our basement adventure.

Outside, I can already hear the drone of gunfire as the first battle of the day begins. What was it like, back in Nathaniel's times, trying to carry on life in this small town while hundreds of thousands of soldiers marched down the main street and barricaded themselves on the surrounding hills and ravines? Knowing Nathaniel now gives those soldiers a human face, a name. Did they feel ready to kill, ready to die? Does anybody?

I blindly grab a plate to serve myself breakfast. I know that most soldiers in the Army of the Potomac were fighting to preserve the Union after the Southern states pulled out. Most in General Robert E. Lee's Army of Northern Virginia fought to preserve the Confederacy, to keep slavery as their way of life. That much I learned in US history last year, even though I read that Lee wasn't all that keen on slavery. But the rest, on both sides? Some were pure abolitionists, totally against slavery, and others were fighting on any which side, just for the adrenaline rush of war. Did they grasp that they might not live through it?

After helping Charlotte clean the guest rooms — she's as easy to chat with as ever, but clams up when I bring up ghosts — I join the masses outside. I'm one of a zillion people gathered around the grassy perimeter of the battlefield. Everybody's slouching in lawn chairs, or huddling on blankets, with their picnic lunches spread around them. A group of kids next to me is running around dripping Popsicle juice and chasing their chocolate Lab. It's a party, not a war.

I watch the reenactors in uniforms on the field. They are rebuilding their barricades with tree limbs and sandbags, slugging back water from sweaty canteens, reloading their muskets, watering their horses, rolling out the cannons. They're aiming at the enemy across the field, waiting for the marshal to call the signal to fire.

The stands are jammed with excited spectators who smell fake blood, waiting for it all to come alive again. Someone's windmilling his arms. Evan. He's motioning me over and squeezing out a spot for me on the bleacher.

"I see you survived the first battle," I tell him.

He tugs at his high collar, smiling. Luck of the draw: He pulled the rank of private in the Confederate army. I can't help but notice that he looks handsome in the gray uniform.

"So far," he says, "one down, but I'm in for a bunch more shoot-outs."

I think of Nathaniel, with a *real* war wound in his back, but Evan is still joking around.

"Lived to tell about the battle, but in a couple days I'll breathe my last in Pickett's Charge when the General himself hollers, 'Charge the enemy and remember Old Virginia!' Funny thing is, I've never been to Virginia, but I'll die in southern glory anyway."

"How many times do you have to die?" I ask dryly.

"Six, all together." He pauses, squinting out at the field The color guard dips the Union flag in front of us to wild applause — thirty-five stars in seven neat rows — and then another regiment dips the Confederate flag, and there's just as much cheering.

"What's it like out there on the field?" I ask.

"Hot. It's not all fun and games. There's lots to remember."

"Such as?"

"You have to keep track of the signals, how far to hang back from the guy in front of you, who to aim at, how and when you're supposed to fall. How to play dead. Out there on the field, you really have to look convincing."

"But what does it actually *feel* like?" I demand, my thoughts on Nathaniel.

Evan's cheeks inflate and he puffs out a giant burst of air. "Feels realistic. I know it's just a show, nobody'll get hurt, and the guys falling dead on the field will be carried out to do it all over again an hour later. But you get caught up in it. Reloading the guns fast as you can. Squinting to get the enemy in your crosshairs, firing at a moving target. The scary thing is, I find myself totally hating the Union soldiers. You gotta have hatred deep in your gut when you shoot to kill, even if you're just shooting blanks." He sinks into himself, and I'm flooded with sympathy for him. Did Nathaniel feel the same way, pumped with hatred, especially when he felt that bayonet thrust?

Evan says, "This is my first year. I'm not doing it next year."

"Smart," I say. Gotta hand it to him. At least he's not as shallow as I'd thought.

"Okay, look," Evan blurts out, and I turn to him, confused. "I'm not the most alert guy on the planet, but I'm picking up that you don't like me. Why not?" Evan is clearly the kind of guy who knows *everybody* likes him.

I'm caught off guard by his question. What does he mean, exactly? Have I been cold toward him? Maybe I've been so distracted by Nathaniel that I'm not even aware of how I'm acting toward the living.

"Well, it's not that I don't like you," I answer truthfully.

"Am I too aggressive? Too pompous? Too friendly? Too adorable?"

"All of the above, except maybe the adorable part."

He smiles broadly, looking, well, reasonably cute. "I might not come back to you with all my parts still attached. How 'bout a kiss for a Reb going off to war?"

I can't help but laugh a little, so I reach over and plant a dry kiss on his cheek. I feel a small tingle of nerves, and also a pang of guilt. But why? In case Nathaniel is watching?

"Lacking passion, but I'm much obliged, Miz Chase," Evan says, holding his gray cap in both hands, like a true southern gentleman.

"When you're back to being the aggressive, pompous, semi-adorable twenty-first century Evan, I need to talk to you about the ever-popular Drydens."

"Right." He nods. "I saw your e-mail this morning. We'll have to talk more after the battle. Why don't you meet me outside the house around two o'clock? I should be done by then." He stands up. "Gives me something to live out the war for."

In my best fake southern accent, I tease, "Y'all be careful, heah?"

Why not? It's July first; everybody plays along.

Evan grins at me. "Count on it, Miz Chase."

Evan has been gone maybe five minutes when an off-duty Union soldier squeezes into a small spot between me and a family of four. I turn, noticing how realistic his blue uniform looks — and it's *him*.

I just stare at Nathaniel, my face flushed with pleasure.

"I'm sorry we had to part ways last night," he tells me. He's murmuring but his voice somehow carries over the roar of the crowd. "I wanted to find you." He doesn't say anything about Evan, so I figure he must not have seen me kiss his cheek. I want to tell Nathaniel I didn't mean it.

I glance around at the spectators and toward the field. "Is it okay for you to do this? Materialize right out in public?"

"It's safe here around hordes of people who look just like me." He smirks to himself. "Most of them don't see me, anyway. You're one of the few. I've practiced every year at this time for longer than a century. It takes so much energy to stay in this bodily form." He throws me a shy glance. "If you hold my hand, I can soak up some of your energy."

"Is that why you were holding my hand so much last night?" I ask, bristling a little. Still, I reach over to put my hand in his, amazed again at how firm and rough his fingers are.

"In part," Nathaniel says, ducking his head. "But I confess I also very much enjoy how it feels."

I lower my own head, blushing furiously.

"Something I've pondered, Lorelei, is why you weren't scared off when I first showed up on your talking machine."

I shake my head. "I *was* scared in the beginning, but you never seemed threatening, really." I think again of that boy I saw in the tree. My séances with Jocelyn.

He nods. "I know. You have the gift. You understand."

I feel a spark of frustration. "But I wish I understood more about you, Nathaniel."

"Yes. We will finish our conversation from last night," he assures me, brushing my palm with his ropy scar. Right now it's as if the whole crowd has vanished. Their noises are dimmed — someone pressed mute — and Nathaniel and I are the only ones sitting on the bleachers, side by side.

Then the bustle of the crowd comes up again at full volume. Fake or not, smoke clouds the air; the sounds reverberate from dozens of bugles and drums and horses, and guns firing all at once. Men cry out in mortal pain; officers shout orders; wounded bodies scramble for shelter; caps fly; flags wave, riddled with bullet holes. It all feels so horribly real.

"Is this what it was like, Nathaniel, deafening and chaotic and terrifying?"

He gazes out over the battlefield, the men rustling around in tense anticipation of the next volley. "I'll tell you what scared us most out there," he begins, drawing in his breath. A ghost drawing breath at all is shocking. "The most terrifying thing wasn't falling in battle, getting shot up, hurting bad. It was dying alone out there, spending all the rest of time alone."

Tears spring to my eyes, and then everything goes quiet on the field, as if every soldier is holding his breath. Nathaniel releases my hand when the next signal is shouted.

"FIRE!"

He whispers in my ear, "Up in the attic, one o'clock." And he's gone; my hand is empty. I jump up, looking for him in the crowd, and people are darting their heads around me so as not to miss a single moment of action. I know I won't see him in this mob. He must have returned to spirit form, and I wonder if he's watching me.

I can't stay here anymore. I stand up and run as fast as the crowd will let me, stepping over blankets and toes and picnic baskets. I have to get out of this scene where war is a jolly spectator sport. In the real world, men and boys as fine as Nathaniel Pierce, who can't possibly be a traitor, fall with bullet-torn bodies and die. Alone.

15

After I come inside, sweaty and overwhelmed, Bertha asks for my help with the dishes. I agree, though I'd rather spend time with Charlotte. But she's already left for the day.

I'm elbow deep in soaking pans, counting the minutes down to one o'clock, when Bertha cries, "Well, lookee here what I found!" She walks over, dangling an old baby's shoe like a dead mouse. "Way in the back of the pantry, kinda lodged into the unfinished part of the wall."

"Looks like a piece of mothy trash to me." And why would she be messing around back there, anyway?

"Trash? Not on your life, missy. It's the concealment shoe. Folks around here always used to put a well-loved child's shoe in the wall when they built. Supposed to hold the spirit of the child and bring good luck to the family. Still waiting for that."

"So," I casually announce, ignoring her comment and turning off the faucet. "I ran into Mr. Dryden in the middle of the night." I haven't mentioned this to my parents yet — I want to investigate it on my own first.

"Couldn't've, unless you were on my sleeping porch on Washington Street. The racket from my old man's loose sinuses kept me up half the night. Musta been some other ugly old man you saw."

She's lying.

"I could be wrong," I say, shrugging.

"There's a lot of that going around," Bertha mutters.

"The hospital that was here before the house was built?"

"What about it?" she grumbles.

"You said some people still hear the cries of wounded soldiers." Like the boys, last night. Can sounds of extreme intensity be stored in a bubble of time that bursts in another century? If I screamed in terror today, would some girl hear it in 2300?

"What do you wanna know?" Bertha asks.

"Anything. I'll tell you when I get bored."

She slams a drawer; silverware clatters inside. "There were makeshift hospitals, here, there, up at the Lutheran Seminary. This was only one of 'em. You could tell which were used as hospitals by the trail of blood up the front steps, and the arms and legs tossed out the back window. Kept dozens of civilians busy just burying the piles of limbs."

Piles of limbs? I'm turning green, swallowing down my nausea.

"Doctors didn't know what to do for splintered bones besides amputate, else the legs would have gone to infection or gangrene and killed the soldiers. Doctors and nurses back then, they hardly knew you had to wash your hands. Didn't have time, anyways, and there wasn't much clean water, with the blood running like an open spigot."

My stomach's doing backflips. "So, most of the soldiers died from gunshot wounds or amputations?" I'm thinking of the jagged bullet hole in Nathaniel's back that killed him.

"From minié-ball shot and cannon-fire balls and bayonet stabbings." Bertha's delighted to share the grim details. "Not the worst of it, though. Disease took more of 'em. Wasn't a pretty time."

"So, why do the locals want to preserve that horror if it was so miserable?"

She shrugs. "It's our history. What's yours?"

The question startles me. "Not war and piles of severed legs," I stammer.

"Anyways, why are you asking me about my old man?" she shoots back.

My turn to shrug. "Okay, I got bored. Talk to you later."

Nathaniel's waiting for me in the attic, so I fly up the stairs, Gertie lapping after me. I've noticed Nathaniel and Gertie seem nervous around each other. Are animals to ghosts like silver daggers to vampires? Another thing I don't know about spirits. Gertie barks at the ceiling door to the attic; she hears something I don't. *Nathaniel.* I open the door a crack, and Gertie backs away, skitters down the stairs. And then the door is pulled open, and Nathaniel's reaching for me.

"You poking your head up like this reminds me of that groundhog you told me about." He smiles; his eyes dance. "Punxsutawney Phil, meet Punxsutawney Nate," and he pulls me up into his arms.

Before I can respond, he lowers his head and kisses me.

Not a quick kiss on the cheek like I gave Evan, but a full kiss on the lips. My first kiss, actually. Who cares that it's with a ghost? It sure feels real. It's sweet and delicious and I want it

to go on and on. I close my eyes and kiss him back, and feel my
insides turn to Jell-O.

Slowly Nathaniel pulls away, studying me with a small
smile. "Forgive me," he says with his usual politeness. "I have
been wanting to do that."

"Same here," I tell him, still dazed, and I realize that *is* just
what I've wanted.

Nathaniel leads me over to the trunk, and we sit on it, facing
each other. I crisscross my legs. I know we're here so Nathaniel
can finish telling me his story. We keep a business-like distance
between us even though all I want is for us to start kissing
again.

"So now you know most of my story," Nathaniel tells me.
"And the question is, who would have wanted to kill me, besides
any one of the eighty-eight thousand Confederate soldiers aiming guns and cannons at me?"

I think back to what Nathaniel told me late last night, in
my room: how, as he lay on his cot bleeding, the doctor and
Henry Baldwin had had a scuffle. Both men had been angry
at him.

"What about Henry Baldwin?" I start. "He had a motive.
He thought you were a traitor."

Nathaniel nods. "Henry was ferocious with grief over his
brother's death, and he blamed me for bringing that Reb boy

in. But he left the tent, I remember. Though it could be he came back."

We think together. I'd rather return to the kissing, where we're in perfect sync, and treason and lies and murder evaporate. I inch a little closer and ask, "What about the doctor, then? He was going crazy about that stolen Lincoln ring, wasn't he? Crazy enough to murder you?"

Nathaniel wets his lips. "I didn't tell you the last of the story. Maybe the ring, Mr. Abraham Lincoln's ring, was Doc's good-luck charm, and maybe it was his curse. Either way you want to believe, the man fell to a random bullet as soon as he stepped outside our tent. I heard all the other soldiers in the tent talking about it when it happened. Just his time, I guess. Or maybe he was murdered, too."

"Oh, come on, another murder? Let's just deal with the one we've got: yours. At least we can cut that doctor from our list of suspects." I think for another minute, chewing on my bottom lip. "So you gave the ring to Wince, right? Before you died?" Suspicion flashes through my mind. "And what did Wince do with the ring then?"

My thoughts are racing. Maybe Wince, Nathaniel's best friend in the regiment, knew the ring was valuable. Valuable enough to take it from Nathaniel, and then shoot him to keep him quiet. Then Wince sold it for a small fortune after the war ended. Maybe he sold it back to President Lincoln. Maybe that's where Wince got the money to build the Vienna Carmody House. My house.

Nathaniel shakes his head, looking stricken. "Are you suspecting Wince of something sinister?" Nathaniel's eyes turn hard. "No. Winston Carmody was the best friend I ever had."

"At least since Edison Larch," I blurt out, remembering his childhood friend. "Didn't you say you thought you saw Edison at the Battle?"

Nathaniel looks thoughtful. The sun streaming in the window shifts and his face is partly hidden, reminding me that as real and present as he seems now, he's actually shadow and smoke. A tiny pinpoint of hope dots my heart: Maybe he's wrong about leaving me when the Battle Days are over. Maybe if I solve the murder, it will somehow keep him *here*. Anything's possible. The laws of the universe are suspended sometimes, aren't they? Newborns who weigh under a pound survive. Tornadoes take out a town, but leave one house standing. People who've been pronounced dead open their eyes and jump-start their lives all over again. Can't a miracle happen just this once?

"I might have imagined Edison being here at Gettysburg," Nathaniel says, looking back at me.

"But Wince *was* here," I press, mentally adding him to the list of suspects.

Nathaniel shakes his head vehemently. "He was a good and loyal friend, Winston Carmody was. I'm certain that he went to the hospital to return the ring and placed it somewhere among Doc's things so no one would ever suspect me of stealing it. He probably left the tent before I was shot."

My shoulders sag. No wonder he's never solved this murder. "We're hitting a wall."

Nathaniel looks around, searching for the wall, and I remember that he's clueless about twenty-first-century slang. I hide my smile.

"Getting nowhere," I explain. I glance at my watch. "And I have to talk to a friend now." For some reason I don't want to tell him that I'm going to ask Evan to explore the basement with me. "Can we meet in the evening, down by the creek?"

He leans over and kisses me again. I guess that means *yes*.

16

I WALK DOWNSTAIRS in a haze — both from Nathaniel's kisses and from thinking about the circumstances of his death. Gertie joins me as I leave the stuffy house and cross the lawn in search of Evan.

I see him, changed out of his uniform into a T-shirt and jeans. He's maneuvering his precious Weedwacker, which is doing its search-and-destroy on dandelions. Gertie and I follow, trying not to sacrifice toes and paws to the rogue weeder.

"So. Drydens, the hot topic of the day?" Evan prompts when he sees me.

I nod, trying to change gears from Nathaniel's tale of bloodshed and mystery to the current topic of conversation.

"How well you know Old Dryden?" I ask, keeping careful to whisper.

"The Hunchback of Notre Doom? On a scale of one to five, with one being we'd nod passing each other at Walmart, and five being we're twins separated at birth, I'd say minus three. He's not a know-worthy man."

"Is he sneaky?"

"Too grouchy to be sneaky." He laughs, and Gertie whips his leg with her wagging tail. "I just contract with him to do the backbreaking work he's too decrepit to do."

"What's he like, really?"

"The guy has no sense of humor. A man without a sense of humor is not to be trusted."

I jump at that. "You don't trust him?"

"I don't *mistrust* him. There's just something fishy, like his brain has a microchip missing."

"That's it perfectly. How many summers have you worked for him?"

Evan turns off the Weedwacker and makes a big show of counting each finger. "Including this summer? One."

"Really?" That doesn't make sense. "Bertha makes it sound like they've been here forever. Like they were *hatched* in the house, like cockroaches, so they have squatters' rights. They're harder to peel away than wallpaper."

Evan raises his eyebrows. "Not so. This is their first season. Where'd you get the idea they were regulars?"

"Bertha said. Implied."

"Lori, you've been snookered."

I shake my head. "But Bertha's a native. She knows so much about Gettysburg and the Battle." I hear her voice in my head: *It's our history. What's yours?*

"Ever hear of Google?" Evan teases. "Though, I don't know, maybe she grew up here. I'll ask my dad. But I've lived here my whole life. She hasn't. A town this size, you recognize everybody, and I never saw her or Old Dryden before April."

I start pacing, my mind racing. Suddenly it seems there's another mystery to unravel besides Nathaniel's murder. "Do you think she's a pathological liar?"

Evan shrugs. "Maybe she and the hubby have something major to hide."

I nod, coming to a stop. "Which might be why I found him crouching under a table in our basement late at night. I was hoping you'd know why."

He shakes his head. "I'm clueless. That's what my three sisters tell me."

I can't help but smile. "Want to come with Gertie and me to explore the basement?" I'm hoping to get down there during daylight hours, and with company — and not of the little McLean boys variety.

"I'd follow Gertie anywhere," Evan says, "as long as you're with her." He grins and turns the Weedwacker on again. "I need to finish up here, then mow the Engles' lawn. Five o'clock, dark and dank cellar?"

Evan's brought a flashlight that's bright enough to scare bats in their cave. Gertie and I follow him down the steps to the basement. Gertie doesn't like it down here. I feel jittery myself. I'm picking up scents I missed before: the lingering rank odor of decay, and something sweet and pungent. It's familiar. I can't place it, but it makes me want to breathe through my mouth, not my nose. Evan's flashlight plays around the corners, revealing nothing new. Gertie zeroes in on the squirrel bones the boys found. But since it's not fresh meat, and the bones are only like twigs, Gertie loses interest.

"Where was Old Dryden?" Evan asks. I motion to the door, which is now closed. "I don't remember closing that door last night, though," I say, feeling spooked.

Evan spots the loose doorknob on the floor and fiddles with the latch. Naturally, the door creaks open, like any self-respecting door in a horror movie.

It's a small back room. The window's blacked out — to prevent anyone looking in and seeing what goes on inside? The flashlight's high beams jump around, spotlighting the gurgling hot-water heater, the giant breaker box that hulks against a wall with all the little levers facing the right direction, the furnace and water pipes snaking up to the ceiling. It's all as it should be, nothing sinister.

Until something brushes the top of Evan's head, and he jumps a foot, jerking the flashlight upward.

"Relax, it's just a pull string for the lightbulb." I yank it, and that's all it takes for the bulb to burn out. If our flashlight battery dies, we're cooked.

"Must be a worktable," Evan observes, illuminating the waist-high ledge bolted to the south wall. It's nicked and stained like it's seen eons of use. A few stray tools and Gerber baby food jars full of nails and screws clutter the end of the table, which has an odd hole in its center, not quite large enough for a softball to sink through.

Evan squats under the table. "There's no trash basket under here to collect things dropped through the hole. Maybe it's to drain turpentine or water or some other fluid."

"Blood." Suddenly it hits me. Didn't Dad and Bertha say this was a hospital? "I think this was an operating table." I think of the doctor Nathaniel met, the one driven to madness because of his missing ring. Patting around underneath the tabletop, I hit a narrow drawer, which I yank but can't force open.

"I don't see a key conveniently hanging on a nearby nail," Evan says, but he hands me a flat-blade screwdriver that fits in the warped wood gap. I'm able to pry the drawer open, smashing the soft old wood a little. Gertie's on her hind legs, champing to see what's inside.

"Forget it, Gertie. All that work for nothing." It's just an empty drawer lined with that brown cloth that keeps silver from tarnishing. I jam the drawer shut, disappointed.

Evan looks over, furrowing his brow. "If the drawer's empty, Lori, why's it locked?"

My fingers probe the bottom of the drawer under the table, snagging on splinters of rough wood. The drawer is deeper than I expected. I pull it open and peel back the brown cloth to find a small compartment of unfinished wood.

And inside is a polished wooden box about a foot long, maybe three inches high. Old-fashioned initials are carved into the box's lid: *RVA*.

I gasp.

"What'd you find?" Evan peers over my shoulder. "Who's RVA?"

"Maybe we'll find out in a sec." A tiny brass knob just begs me to pull out the box's small drawer. My hands are clammy with dread as I slide the drawer open, expecting to see — what? — insect carcasses? Piles of Confederate greenbacks? An ivory elephant tusk? None of the above. Inside, cradled in red velvet niches, are five small, rusty knives with ivory handles. Knives like nothing you'd see in a kitchen, nothing you'd see in the twenty-first century. I quickly slide the small drawer shut and run my finger over the carved initials, RVA, wondering who he is, or was. Shaking, I unclasp the latch and throw the lid open. There's a small handsaw inside, rusted and jagged-edged. Gertie wants to lick it, but I shoo her away.

Suddenly, Old Dryden's words last night echo in my head: *Doctor only needed twelve minutes to cut off a whole leg. Arm, less than that.* Now I realize why he was saying that.

"I know what this is, Evan. It's an amputation kit."

"No way. Let me see." He flicks his finger over the rusty edge of a knife. "It must have seen a lot of action, because this thing wouldn't cut through a chunk of cheddar."

I squirm. "This is what Old Dryden was looking for, I'm sure of it." I'm feeling more creeped out by the minute. "But why?"

"The old Hunchback of Notre Doom must be planning to do some amateur surgery."

I shake my head, mystified and horrified. "I'm taking the kit upstairs to hide until we can figure out what it's all about."

"Maybe I'll do a little online research." Evan looks pensive, and I can tell that he's as spooked by this find — locked drawer, rusty old knives, amputation — as I am. I wonder if I should ask Nathaniel about this discovery, if he would know any more than we do.

Gertie is starting to whine; she wants out. "Let's go." We close the door and tiptoe up the rickety stairs. While Evan ushers Gertie into the kitchen, I dash up to my room with the box, stashing it inside the case of an extra pillow on my bed. As I'm coming back downstairs, something that's been murky in my mind suddenly runs clear. It's like when a tune coils through your brain, but you just can't pull out the title until you're doing something mindless, like sweeping cobwebs off the ceiling. Now I recognize that sweet, pungent smell from the basement. I know it from biology, from frog dissection. It's chloroform, a drug that can knock people unconscious. Why is that scent wafting through our cellar?

17

FROM THE KITCHEN window, Evan and I watch Gertie run around outside. The yard looks innocent enough in the yellowish late-afternoon glow. Up the hill's the lawn-mower shed. Just a small barnlike building covered in pine boards, new but built to look old. Why did it feel so threatening the other night?

The garden sprinkler is hissing. Old Dryden's kitchen garden is a riot of color, overflowing with radishes and cucumbers, peppers and zucchini, leafy herbs and vining tomato plants. And then I can't stop my awful thought: Is it such a bountiful crop because of creepy Dryden's loving, stoop-backed care? Or because this ground has been fertilized by so many human remains of the 1863 Battle?

Thankfully Evan interrupts my thoughts. "Let's go down to the creek," he says. "I want to talk to you about something."

"Sounds ominous," I tease, while inside I feel my stomach give a jump. We step outside and I whistle to Gertie. "Come on, Gertie Girl, water sports!"

She beats us down the hill and dives in like a water nymph while we wade in the shallow near the bank. Evan's not talking, and I'm curious. I wish-wish-wish Nathaniel's shimmery image would appear, but it's just Evan beside me.

About halfway across the creek, Gertie's head juts up out of the water, and she growls ferociously.

"What's up, girl?" Maybe a water snake spooked her. She's not usually that skittish. She swims back to me, her growl reduced to a low rumble. I love the smell of wet dog.

"So, I was wondering," Evan says, like it's a continuation of a chat we've been having all day. "There's a thing tonight up at Herr Ridge."

"What kind of thing?"

"A ball."

Gertie wags her tail. *Ball* is one of her top ten words.

"Like a dance ball," Evan elaborates. "Wanna go?"

I'm taken aback. I think of how many times I used to wish that Danny Bartoli would ask me to a school dance. He never did. Is Evan . . . asking me out?

"I'm not really a . . . ball kind of girl," I explain. Plus, I'm supposed to meet Nathaniel later. I can't miss that.

"Great, so I'll come by and get you at nine o'clock." Evan grins at me, and I laugh despite myself.

"Try to scare up a nineteenth-century ball gown," he adds. "Plus white gloves, parasol, the whole shebang." He reaches across Gertie and winds my hair into a bun up on the crown of my head. I'm surprised by the sudden contact, but I don't mind it. "Nice locks for an upsweep 'do, a few tendrils on the side, maybe?"

I shake my hair loose. "What do you know about hair-dos, Evan?"

"Three sisters, don't forget. Our shower dispenses hot-and-cold conditioner instead of water."

I sigh. "I don't know, Evan. Where am I supposed to find an antique ball gown in, like, four hours?"

He laughs. "I'll bet Charlotte has something you can borrow. All the women around here have Civil War stuff hanging in their closets. I'll ask my sisters." He steps back in the water to look me over. "One's about your size."

"No! Did I say I was going?"

Evan runs a hand through his shaggy blond hair. "You know what you are, Lori Chase? You're a fuddy-duddy."

"What's a fuddy-duddy?" I feel like Nathaniel, lost in unknown words.

"A stick-in-the-mud, a Gloomy Glinda."

I snort. "Well, at least Glinda was the *good* witch in Oz. What was the bad witch's name? Doesn't matter; she's not going to the dance, and neither am I."

Evan laughs, nudging me. "Hey, lighten up, Lori. You're entitled to time off for good behavior. See if Charlotte has a fan, too. Fans are fetching."

Fetch, another one of Gertie's top vocab words. She trots over with high expectations, so Evan throws a stick across the lawn. Gertie races for it and brings it back in her mouth. Her eyes plead: *Again? Again!*

I guess I have been a little preoccupied with ghosts and murder and amputated limbs as of late. Mom's been urging me to get out and have some fun. Here's my big chance. "Nine o'clock, yeah, okay." I'll meet Nathaniel afterward, I decide. "But it's not a date."

"Noooo. It's a nice guy taking a beautiful girl to a ball on a moonlit summer night. Doesn't sound like a date to me, either."

A blush burns my cheeks and I look down. Evan thinks I'm beautiful? Does Nathaniel?

"I think you're beautiful, too," comes a warm, familiar voice in my ear. I look around, but no one is there besides Evan, and he's busy jogging over to Gertie, who's halfway across the lawn. The voice comes again. "I've always been partial to tall, brown-haired ladies who speak their mind."

My heart is racing and I'm trying to fight my blush. I wait until Evan is out of earshot until I whisper, "Nathaniel! I thought you weren't going to spy on me or do the invisible number, remember?" But the truth is, I don't mind anymore.

"How could I resist this time? He's taking you to a fancy-dress ball." Just like that, Nathaniel shimmers into the space before my eyes, taking on his solid form. I hear Gertie across the lawn starting to bark like crazy — she must sense Nathaniel's presence — but Evan distracts her by tossing the stick again. They can't see us.

Nathaniel sighs, looking disappointed. "Since you will be otherwise occupied at our appointed meeting time, might you stay here now so we can talk?" He jerks his head in Evan's direction. "Hopefully he will leave you be for a while."

"You're jealous!" I soften my whisper. "I can't believe it."

"Believe what?" Evan asks, jogging over with a barking Gertie at his heels.

In a flash, Nathaniel disappears, and I'm left stammering.

"I didn't say *believe*," I lie, glancing at Evan. "I said bee — beehive."

Nathaniel laughs in my ear.

Evan frowns. "I haven't seen bees around. A few wasps, maybe." He shrugs. "So, I'll come by at nine, okay?" Evan waves to me, then starts back up the lawn toward his car. Gertie runs panting after him, and thankfully, he pauses to let her back into the house.

"Nathaniel? Are you still there?" I whisper.

I stand and wait in the gathering evening. It's weirdly quiet; not even the whistling song of cicadas in the trees. The musky smell of decaying leaves wafts up from the creek, not unpleasantly. Lights blink on in one room up at the house as a guest comes back from dinner. Ms. Wilhoit, I think. Shadows have started to lengthen under the trees around me.

"You look magical in the fading light of day, like a fairy princess," Nathaniel says, materializing by my side.

I wish I could stop blushing. I'm not sure what to do with all these compliments.

"A princess in a Phillies T-shirt and cutoff jeans," I say. He has no idea what the Phillies are, or even what jeans are, but I wonder if his otherwordly eyes see something different in me.

"So, this Evan Maxwell is taking you to a ball," Nathaniel says, and he sweeps off his hat, pressing it to his chest. "This maims my tender heart."

I want to throw my arms around him but I resist. I catch sight of the elderly Mrs. Crandall on the porch, yellow in the fake kerosene lamplight that's trying to brighten the dusk. Her knitting needles click.

I turn back to Nathaniel, keeping my voice low. "I wish *you* were taking me. But let's meet at the creek after the dance — before midnight. That'll get me through the evening."

"I'll be there." Does he mean the creek, or the dance?

"Listen," I whisper, "I found a strange box — a kit, really —"

Then I hear footsteps and the hair on the back of my neck stands up. Who's coming? Who'll see Nathaniel? I turn around and spot Mr. Crandall in an old-fashioned neck-to-knees swimsuit.

"Evening, Miss Lori," he says. "Thought I'd take a little dip before the sun's gone."

He jumps into the water, feetfirst, swims the length of the creek and back, then rises out of the water with leaves and muck clinging to him. "Ahhh! That was refreshing. Carry on, folks!" and he drips his way up the hill toward the house.

Folks? He sees someone here besides me? Nathaniel hasn't moved. I'm surprised he didn't do his vanishing act when Mr. Crandall appeared.

Before I can ask Nathaniel about this, I see the McLean boys coming our way. Max, the six-year-old, is choking a brown paper bag and shouting, "We're gonna feed the ducks! Mrs. Hannah in the kitchen gave us her stale toast."

"This isn't a pond — there are no ducks here," I start to say, and this time, I see, Nathaniel's an undulating image, like a flag waving in a brisk breeze. He's going.

The boys don't seem to notice anything strange; they just tromp closer to the bank, looking in vain for ducks.

As I start back toward the house, I hear Nathaniel faintly say, "Try not to have too good a time at the ball tonight."

18

I HAVE JUST an hour to transform myself from the softball double-play queen into Scarlett O'Hara. You'd think I was a bride the way Mom and Charlotte are fussing over me up in my room. Hannah's been imported for the Extreme Makeover, too. She can mold bread dough into every-which shape, so apparently she can stuff this five-foot-eight girl into Charlotte's mother's gown.

Patiently, Hannah instructs me to step into the gold, poufy dress. I do so, and the ridiculous hoop skirt and layers of petticoat make the hem stick out like a parachute. The sleeves, which are cinched and flared at the elbows, have enough fabric in them to cover a sofa. And the buttons tracking down the back? Don't ask. My three attendants nip and tuck and tug and tie and button and safety-pin me until I'm all encased in the Civil War–era number. I watch myself in awe in the floor-length mirror. Already, I'm transforming into someone from a different time.

Next, my team goes into hyperdrive on my makeup and hair.

"I need tendrils," I explain, remembering what Evan had said.

"Of course you do," Hannah says, wielding a curling iron like a hand mixer. I smell frying hair. Charlotte's got hair clips and bobby pins between her lips. They're disappearing at an alarming rate into the bird's nest on top of my head. Mom sprays about a quart of hair spray on the whole mess, until it's stiff as copper wire. If I scratch my head, the whole structure tilts. Hannah hands me a knitting needle and says, "Here, this'll dig down into the nest without dislodging it. It's a bit like spun sugar, isn't it? Lovely."

Mom demonstrates how to casually rest a pink parasol on my shoulder and twirl it alluringly, while Charlotte thrusts an ivory fan in my other hand and whispers in my ear, "This ball will take your mind off you-know-who."

The moony, romantic girl in the mirror is definitely not me. I want the plain old Lori back, the cynical one who wise-cracks and used to wear pajama bottoms and flip-flops to Starbucks with Jocelyn. And I don't really want my mind off Nathaniel.

"Oh, Lori," Mom says with tears in her eyes. "You look so . . ."

"Stupid?"

"No, honey. You look utterly gorgeous." She opens the door and yells for Dad. "Vernon, come see what Lori's turned into!"

Dad pokes his head into my room. He's carrying a plunger, having just unstopped General Buford's toilet. His face lights up.

"Why, Lorelei Cordelia, you look stunning."

"Don't bring that drippy plunger in here," Mom cries.

Which reminds me: The neckline of this gown plunges a lot more than I'm used to. That, and tendrils, all on the same night. Too much.

Mrs. Crandall stops by to see the spectacle I've become and says, "Observe everything at the ball, dear girl. Every little thing." Sounds almost like a threat, but then she beams like the grand-mother of the bride and hands me a paper-thin handkerchief. "Dipped in rosewater," she explains. "Makes the gents swoon."

"I need some time to get used to the new, improved Lori before Evan gets here," I plead, and my bevy of attendants take the hint. Besides, Charlotte has to go home and get dressed for the ball herself.

As soon as they're gone, I flip open my laptop. The corset and dress won't let me sit. The hoop pops up over my face. Back in 1863, what did girls do with all this superstructure when they had to go to the bathroom, or even sit down? Well, I'll stand up and type my message to Jocelyn, not that I can actually bend from the waist, either, without being stabbed by plastic stays, buttons, and pins. Good thing I have long arms like an orangutan.

LoriC@squareone.com
You there? what are you up to?

JocelynJ@squareone.com
*my cabin girls have poison ivy! I gotta
slather them w/calamine every 2 hrs. I
signed up to muck out stables, not spread
muck on little twerps.*

LoriC@squareone.com
Get this. I'm going to a fancy-dress ball
tonite. You ought to see me, Jos. I'm a
freakin' Scarlett O'Hara. Rhett's picking me
up in a few.

JocelynJ@squareone.com
is rhett the blond god i didn't get 2 meet?
he obviously likes you! or r u still hanging
around w/the ghost??

This isn't the time to tell her how I'm obsessed with
Nathaniel Pierce and . . . that I don't know how I feel about
Evan. Thankfully, Jos writes back before I can respond:

gotta run get some more calamine. send me
pix of yourself all dressed up!

I'm still thinking about what Jocelyn said when Mom
knocks on my door.

I spin around, and the dress takes a few seconds to catch up
with me. "Come in!" I call.

She sweeps into the room. "Miss Lorelei? There's a dashing
Rebel soldier waiting for you in the parlor."

I'm careful going down the stairs in my giant contraption of
a dress, and my heart skips a beat when I see Evan down in the
foyer, dazzling in his Confederate uniform. He must have had it
dry-cleaned, because it doesn't look muddy like it did earlier in
the day, at the Battle. He's not exactly Rhett Butler, but he looks

almost elegant, his strong jaw lifted proudly, the southern aristocrat. Very different from my Union soldier, Nathaniel.

Mom pats his shoulder. "You're quite a dapper Rebel," she says, and Dad, who's traded the plunger for a camera, is snapping photos. You'd think this was a senior prom in another century. When Evan stands close enough for a good shot, the hoop of the dress jerks to the other side and juts out like a small circus tent. Gertie sticks her snout under the hoop, trying to figure out what this contraption is, so we get a great shot of the three of us — Evan, me, and Gertie's rump.

Even I have to admit that the ballroom at the Inn at Herr Ridge looks magical, with electric sconces designed to look like gaslights, and everything gold-tipped. The crystal chandeliers cast amber lights around the room, which is filled with women in ball gowns as wide as mine, and men decked out in fine blue and gray uniforms.

Raising my fan demurely in front of my face, I whisper to Evan, "Will we southerners stick out like sore thumbs? Looks like mostly Union people here."

"Don't worry about it. Back in the day, Herr Ridge was the CSA hospital."

"Lots of amputations, huh?"

Evan grins. "You're funny."

"For a fuddy-duddy, you mean. Actually, I'm a Scorpio. Scorpios are very passionate."

"Good news!"

"About certain things," I add, giving him a look.

Evan wheels me to the dance floor, where my hoop keeps bumping into other women's hoops. He puts his arm around me in the classic dance frame position, the kind you only see on TV, and I just hope he doesn't accidentally loosen any of the safety pins holding my dress together.

"So," Evan says, smiling. "This is sort of a celebration for me. I got some good news today. A thick envelope from Stanford."

I smile up at him. "You got your first choice!"

"Yep." He beams. "Full ride, too. I worked my way up to the top of the waiting list. My mother's at home weeping like her sinuses are on fire and wailing, 'My baby boy's going so far away!'"

"Mothers. Mine will be blubbering, too, next year this time. Maybe I'll go someplace out of state, Maryland or Connecticut, but not as far as California."

Evan pulls me a little closer; my dress rustles and my voluminous sleeve catches on the epaulettes at his shoulder. "We seem to be attached," I say, trying to disentangle my sleeve.

"It's okay. I like you close."

So we dance like that until the music stops and I wrestle my sleeve loose. The musicians strike up another tune, and we dance and dance. Everything's starting to relax inside as Evan and I waltz — *waltz!* — around the beautifully polished dance floor, sailing past the musicians like graceful ships. He's a smooth dancer, so easy to follow, so easy to be with, so . . . *nice.* No complications. I'm actually feeling very girly all done up this way, as long as I don't try to breathe. My eyes check out the ballroom, taking in the handsome soldiers and ladies of all ages and shapes and sizes gliding in swaying ball gowns. It's like a dream.

Charlotte's across the room in a massive pink birthday cake of a dress. Her hair is done up in two enormous cinnamon-roll braids, one pinned high over each ear. How many bobby pins does it take to anchor those pounds of hair? This is my first glimpse of her boyfriend, Eddie, who's here as a Union cavalry-man. He's no dancer, the way he's tilting her left and right, like a steering wheel, but she looks happy.

And then I spot *him* leaning against the wall, with his booted foot crossed over the other and his eyes fixed squarely on me. People walk past him, *through* him. I'm the only one who sees Nathaniel Pierce, and it doesn't even seem odd anymore. He gives me a bitter smile — Angry? Jealous? — then turns to go. He's a magnet and I'm nothing but a pile of iron filings poured into a Civil War dress. It takes all my energy to resist following him as he slips out of the ballroom.

"What happened?" Evan asks. "You went catatonic." He gently gets me moving again, weaving me through the crowded dance floor. I wonder if Nathaniel is still on the grounds at Herr Ridge, but I figure running out after him might prove futile.

Then, all at once, something strange happens. The room suddenly seems twice as crowded. Shouldn't we be bumping into people left and right? But we're not. Evan leads me past, *through*, other dancers whose gowns are faded, dangling bits of torn lace. They smell of mothballs. The accordion pleats in their fans rest flat on the shoulders of their partners, Rebs and Yanks both, in tattered uniforms. The dancers' feet glide as though there's a cushion of air on the dance floor, like an air hockey table.

My heart is thumping. "Evan? Do you notice anything creepy about some of these couples?"

He shifts his weight away from me, looking at people on both sides. "Like what?"

"They seem to be dancing to different music from what we're hearing."

"Well, yeah, some people have no rhythm. I'm one of them, but my sisters made me learn to dance because they said I'd never get a girlfriend if I kept clunking. How am I doing?"

"Fine, great," I murmur, stunned that he doesn't see what I see.

Because they're ghosts. Did Nathaniel somehow cause this . . . hallucination? But these people seem so real. One woman sashays past me and whispers in my ear, "We all look forward to your joining us."

I feel my blood run cold. *Joining them?* As in . . . dying? "No!" I shout, and Evan stretches out his arm that's held mine close to his chest.

"Sorry," he grumbles. "I thought you liked it."

"No, it's not you. It's them. The others." He has no clue what I'm talking about, but he creates more space between our bodies. I stare at the gliding ghosts over Evan's shoulders, fascinated, until one by one they blink out and the dance floor's no more crowded than it was two minutes ago. A shudder ripples through me.

"Evan, I'm dying of thirst." Poor choice of words. He's irritated, I can tell, but he steers me to the punch bowl, moving us in time to the music. I guess he's learned something about rhythm after all.

The punch smells like cotton candy and is a ghastly Hi-C red. Also, I'm known to be a klutz. Better not drip any on Charlotte's mother's gown. I'm hungry so I pop stuffed mushrooms into my mouth as we're joined by Evan's friend Barry. He's dressed in a uniform identical to Nathaniel's, but he's not nearly as handsome. The two of them talk about Stanford — the tradition of people diving into the many fountains on campus, and the traditional primal screams before finals — but now I want to scream. I can't stop thinking about Nathaniel. And then I realize the time.

"Evan, sorry, but I have to go, now."

He scrunches up his face, seeing the sudden urgency in mine. Glancing at his watch, he says, "Whoa, it's eleven o'clock. Yeah, we need to get going. I'm in three battles tomorrow, and I have to die again in Pickett's Charge. See ya, Barry."

Outside, he asks, "What's the big hurry? You've been out past ten once or twice in your life, right? Not like you're gonna turn into a werewolf or anything. Man, it's complicated hanging with you, Lori."

"So why do you?" I ask, trying to stuff my entire gigantic dress in the front seat of his Camaro. The hoop pops up and covers the dashboard. Evan has to shove it toward my window so he can see.

"Hey, right, that's what I'm wondering, myself. Speculation: because the new girl in town's a challenge?"

I hug the door in stony silence.

He turns off the ignition in the middle of the deserted country road. "Okay, what's changed suddenly, Lori? We were having a good time ten minutes ago."

"What do you mean, what's changed?" But I know what he means. He senses that I'd come closer, but now was drifting away from him, and it's true.

"I don't get it. Get you. You're like a faulty tap, running hot and cold. Where's the passionate Scorpio you warned me about?"

"Sorry, Evan. I'm just tired. A lot's been going on this week. The basement, the shed, all that stuff. I just need to get some sleep."

At Coolspring Inn, he parks, ready to jump out, but I thank him and give him a kiss on the cheek that sort of misses and brushes his ear. "Don't get out. I'll talk to you tomorrow, okay? Thanks for a nice evening."

"Yeah, right," he mutters.

"Have a good death on the battlefield tomorrow," I call from the porch. He waits until I unlock the front door and wave from inside before he pulls away.

I run upstairs to get out of this uncooperative monster of a dress as fast as I can. The gauzy petticoats and the hoop skirt slide down easily enough. But the twenty-seven seed-pearl buttons down the back — yes, we counted twenty-seven — are impossible to undo quickly. How did they ever undress back then? I decide to leave the dress on for my visit to the creek. I hurry downstairs. Without the hoop, the dress brushes my toes. I kick off the stacked heels and run barefoot, holding the skirt up so it doesn't drag through the wet grass. It's beautiful tonight with moonlight reflecting on the water like drizzled fresh cream.

He's there, leaning against the wrought-iron bench facing the creek. A full moon lights his face. His dark eyes gleam. I am completely in his power. He tucks my arm across his, and I melt like chocolate as we stroll through the wet grass. The bottom of my dress is soaked now, but the wrappings around his leg are not. Is he here, solid flesh, or isn't he? If it rained, would he be dry? If an apple falling from a tree hit his head, would he feel it? Or can he only feel the old wounds? Nathaniel does seem to feel my arm locked in his. He pats my hand and again a chill feathers up my arm. What's totally weird is that I've never before felt so alive as I do right now with this person who's dead.

"You are right comely," he says, looking over the whole costume. "Just like a girl from my day. Prettier than any."

"Thank you, Nathaniel." I can't but smile at his words. "So, I wonder, why did you come to the ball?"

"I wanted to see you," he says. "You looked happy . . . with *him*," he adds resentfully.

I realize that it was really Nathaniel who made me see all those ghosts around me. But why? As punishment? I'm flattered that he's jealous, but I feel a pang of annoyance. Does Nathaniel not expect me to have any friends who are, oh, I don't know, alive? I think of how hurt Evan looked in the car dropping me off.

"Nathaniel," I say sharply, "you can't control everything I do. I'm not a Muppet." I feel silly saying it.

"Another thing in your world I do not know."

"A — a hand puppet." I chew my bottom lip. "Never mind."

"Like a Punch and Judy show."

"Who are they?" I ask.

"Punch and Judy were puppets popular in my time. My father made us a puppet stage, and Edison and I used to put on shows for our neighbors in Punxsutawney."

I try to picture that, Nathaniel as a boy, wagging puppets around on a stage. It doesn't work. In my world, he's eternally nineteen.

"Forgive me, Lorelei. I'm desperate, and time is running out."

"I know, Nathaniel," I say, softening. "But I don't know if we can solve your mystery in the next two days. It's what we call today a cold case. No clues left."

Nathaniel's eyelids flutter; as he said earlier today, I've *maimed his heart*. "It is not a cold case to me, Lorelei. The trail's warmed since you came to Gettysburg. The clues are there. You just need to see them and follow them. Believe me, I've tried to do it myself through these centuries. Time has played tricks on me. The time is now. You are the key."

I feel frustrated, and the twenty-seven buttons digging into my back don't help. "I can't unlock a thing!" I cry. "Everything I stumble across just confuses me more. Edison, Wince, the doctor, Henry Baldwin. It's all a muddle."

"Let us sit, Lorelei." He brushes off a few leaves and pats the bench.

I gather the big skirt, which is much more manageable without the bothersome infrastructure of petticoats, and fold the gold fabric between my knees.

"Okay," I say, trying to think like a detective. "Let's talk about motive. If the doctor was killed right after he left you, it doesn't matter that he thought you had his ring. But Henry Baldwin thought you were a traitor. And I can't" — I cast a cautious look at Nathaniel — "I can't stop thinking about Edison. He felt betrayed. You know that. He sent you that letter.

Maybe he'd been looking for you all this time. He came into the tent and saw his opportunity."

Nathaniel frowns. "But we don't know for certain if he was at the Battle. I just thought I'd glimpsed him."

I nod. "Maybe I can do a little research, see if I can find that Edison was here."

Nathaniel is silent for a moment, watching me. Then he murmurs, "I don't have much time to solve my, as you say, cold case, but there is one thing I'd like to do now."

"What?" I ask. He whispers, "I'm determined to dispel all memories of your evening at Herr Ridge."

I jerk back. "Can you do that? Can spirits actually erase someone else's memories? That would be awful and —"

"No, that's not within my limited powers, but maybe this will be a start." He pulls me toward him, locks me in his arms, and his lips on mine are warm and firm. They taste of ginger, and I can't get enough.

19

THE NEXT MORNING, Evan's down on the lawn, clipping at some low branches, though not very energetically. I know he's supposed to be at the Battle site soon, but it could be he's hanging around Coolspring awaiting an apology for my revolting behavior last night. I owe that to him, for sure, and as I watch him down there, I get an idea. I stayed up very late last night, sitting with Nathaniel by the creek, kissing and whispering about the night of his murder. But we didn't get any closer to an answer. Maybe it's time for a second opinion.

I knock on my window, signaling to Evan to wait for me.

Downstairs, I drop four of Hannah's oatmeal raisin cookies into a plastic bag.

Not a word from Evan as I get close.

"Sorry about last night. I brought you cookies. Peace offering."

He takes my little baggie, pops a whole cookie in his mouth. "Not bad. You baked them?" His words are all muffled by smushed cookie.

"Hannah. I'm the world's worst baker, and besides, who's had time? I've been busy ruining a fancy-dress ball." A sideways glance lets him know that I'm teasing, and I watch him make a split-second decision to quit being mad at me. He really is a very forgiving guy. He even offers me half of the last cookie.

Mouth full of crumbs, I mumble, "You're practically a Stanford guy, which means you're way smart, so I need to pick your brain."

Evan drills an imaginary doorway into his head. "Does this have something to do with the packet of dull knives?"

"Maybe. I don't know yet." I take a deep breath. "So. A few days ago I went on one of those ghost tours, you know?"

"Woooooooo!" He trills his fingers and does a great job of rolling his eyes around in his head.

"Yeah, a little cheesy, but people around here seem to see ghosts all over the place."

"The tourists do, not the regulars. Me, for instance. I've lived in Gettysburg all my life and have never seen, heard, or felt a ghostly presence. We don't sit around the dinner table talking about evil spirits like it's all Halloween, all the time."

"But some people . . ."

"Are you one of them?" he asks, frowning.

Can I trust him? "No judgments, okay? This may sound crazy."

"Keep talking. I'll just drop these clippers in the shed so we can jog down to the road."

The shed. Just hearing him mention it makes me itchy. What *is* it about that place? "Can you leave the clippers here and stash them away later?"

He reads something in my eyes. His face tightens into concern as he lays the clippers under a bench. "Sure, let's go."

The road below Coolspring is unpaved and quiet, with overgrown fields on both sides. "You could pay for college mowing those fields," I tease, trying to keep it light and airy before I delve into the darker depths of what's going on.

"But they're just the way Mother Nature wants them, with those bee balm wildflowers and the blueweed." I hadn't even noticed the flowers; just the wild grass. What kind of a person am I to see ghosts and totally miss a field of wildflowers?

"So, you were saying — ghosts?" he asks.

I nod, choosing my words carefully. "Last night at the dance, you probably didn't notice. There were dozens of them on the dance floor."

"Dozens of . . . ?" He looks dubious.

"Ghosts," I finish for him.

He nods, but it's clear he doesn't believe me.

"And I've made friends with one," I blurt. "With an actual ghost." *A lot more than friends.* "He's a soldier."

Evan pulls himself taut beside me, clearly uncomfortable with this idea, but he doesn't say anything.

"He was murdered here in 1863."

"Nobody gets 'murdered' in the middle of a battle with bullets and cannonballs flying."

"Wrong. He was murdered. And he wants me to figure out who did it."

Evan strokes his chin as if there's actually a little beard there. He's trying to figure out what to say without telling me that I need to be committed to a psych ward.

"You promised no judgments," I remind him.

"I did, yes. So, keep going."

"A lot of odd things have been going on since I got here. Old Dryden sneaking into our cellar. The Drydens lying about being old-timers here. And then there's the person who was snooping around in the shed, and don't tell me it was a raccoon.

I *saw* someone running out the back door. To be honest, the shed sends creepy vibes down my spine. That's why I didn't want you to put the clippers away."

"You think the shed is haunted?" Evan asks, trying hard not to mock me.

"I don't know. Sometimes I think an evil living person can be a lot scarier than a ghost. Call me a sensitive, an intuitive, a nut, whatever, but I'm picking up signals most people miss. You miss." I glance over to see if he's insulted. He seems thoughtful, mulling over all this bizarre stuff I've said, so I continue.

"It's a giant jigsaw puzzle in my mind, and I'm trying to fit all the pieces together, including the RVA box with the knives. What if it has something to do with Nathaniel?"

"Nathaniel?" he asks quietly.

"The soldier I told you about."

"The one who was murdered."

"Yes." It sounds preposterous out here on this dirt road with beautiful wildflowers all around us.

"That surgical kit, I'm sure it's left over from the Battle," I say, trying to reason out what I've been thinking.

"Don't forget, though," Evan cuts in, "the house wasn't even built until about fifteen years afterward."

"I know, but the foundation's original and the ground under the house *was* a field hospital," I say. "I'm thinking someone dug this surgical kit up and hid it in the house much later. I think it's what Old Dryden was looking for. Maybe it's why he and Bertha came to this house in the first place."

"Wow, an antique amputation kit must be worth an arm and a leg," Evan says, and we both laugh. "A little dark humor for comic relief," he adds, grinning. "So, why's the Hunchback looking for it?"

"No idea. We need to find out who RVA was. Also, Nathaniel told me something about a ring that mysteriously disappeared, that belonged to some doctor. Too many loose pieces to pull together into one picture."

A car crawls by. I can't see who's inside, but I get a hair-raising feeling that whoever it is is looking us over. The license plate is from Massachusetts. Must be a tourist, but why would a casual tourist care about two kids walking up a dusty road?

"Does that car creep you out?" I ask anxiously.

"Nah. They're just admiring the scenery."

"What if *we're* the scenery?" I frown as Evan shakes his head. "Don't say it; you think I'm paranoid."

"I didn't say it."

The car slowly backs up. It's the Crandalls, and now Mrs. Crandall's waving a blue handkerchief out the window.

"Halloo! Look here, Earl, it's Lori and the lawn boy!"

Mr. Crandall toots the horn and speeds ahead.

There's a house up the road with a sign that says HOLLOWAY'S HIDEAWAY. "Let's duck up this way," Evan suggests. "I know the family here." I'm relieved that Evan's familiar with all the out-of-the-way places in Gettysburg. So we head toward the clapboard house. Bikes and riding toys clutter the grass, and two little girls are splashing in a plastic pool.

"Hey, Judy and Fiona," Evan says. "How's it going?"

"EvanBevanSpevanDevan!" one of the girls yells, scooping out handfuls of water to splash in his face.

"Watch it, ladies, you're drowning me. Retaliation!" He reaches in and splashes them back, sending them into giggles. Meanwhile, I look down the driveway and see that the Crandalls' car is stalled at the end. Waiting for us?

"Okay with you ladies if we sit here on your porch?" Evan asks.

One of the girls squeals and shouts, "Mommy, Evan's here with some girl." The *some girl* part sounds a little snide.

The porch steps are wide and out of earshot of the pool.

Quickly, I fill Evan in on my thoughts about Nathaniel's murder and the possible motive.

Evan tilts his head to one side, thinking. "Could it be that the murderer was jealous? That he and this Nathaniel person loved the same girl?"

"No, I don't think so," I reply quickly, and he gives me a searching look that makes me blush.

"Or how about revenge for something Nathaniel did to him or to somebody he loved. Your guy seem like a baddie?"

"No, squeaky clean to the core." Nathaniel would never do anything to hurt a soul.

"Like you·can tell in two or three days," Evan mutters.

"I'm an excellent judge of character," I shoot back.

"Okay, don't bite my head off."

"I mean, Nathaniel was battle-weary and exhausted after the first day, and he still brought a wounded kid into the hospital, a Confederate soldier. He could have left him to die, but he didn't."

"Got it. He was a saint. Next theory: Could it be a personal vendetta? Someone who had something against him?"

"Exactly," I say. "That's why I keep coming back to Edison."

"The lightbulb guy?"

"No, Edison Larch. Nathaniel's friend growing up. I just have to prove that he was here at the Battle."

Evan shakes his head. "I don't follow, but if you say so; okay. And by the way, apology accepted about last night."

• • •

After Evan and I part ways, I go back to the inn to track down Charlotte. I need to find out what she knows about Nathaniel. She recognized him on the ghost tour, but she hasn't opened up to me about it since. Why? Maybe they have some sort of history. I hope he didn't turn to her first before I showed up in Gettysburg. But he would have mentioned her to me then, right?

I dial her number and find out from her mother that Charlotte's got the one-to-nine shift tonight at the Blue Parrot Restaurant. I'm pacing, chewing my knuckles, picking at an old scab on my knee — squirmy restlessness. It feels like the hour before last season's championship game when my Liberty Bells uniform felt too tight, and my arm felt too loose, and my catcher's glove suddenly didn't fit my hand anymore.

Two hours pass, and I try Charlotte's number again. Her little brother answers and bellows, "CHARLEY!!! PHONE!!!" She'd warned me about her rambling house with all those kids and dogs and hamsters and a warren of rabbits in the yard, not to mention a ferret Charlotte's sister got for her tenth birthday.

Charlotte picks up an extension. "Hello?"

"Hi, Charlotte. It's me. Lori."

"Oh, hi!" Charlotte sounds pleased to hear from me, which is a relief. I was wondering if she'd really been distancing herself from me. She asks me if I had a good time at the dance, and

I say I did, without mentioning what happened afterward.
Then I launch right into my mission.

"Nathaniel Pierce. Can you tell me more about him?"

"Not much to tell." Charlotte sounds evasive, and I wonder
if she's a little in love with him, too. She says, "He shows up
every year at this time, but he only stays until the Battle Days
are over. Honestly? It surprised me to see him. He's usually just
spirit, not flesh. You must be special for him to appear in bodily
form and give you his name. Once a spirit offers his name, he's
vulnerable. He's yours."

Mine? My heart thuds. He certainly feels like mine, in a
way. "Well, we've been talking every day," I confess. I don't tell
her about the kissing. "But honestly, I'm out of my league here.
Nothing like this has ever happened to me before." Well, except
for the boy who fell from the tree, and Great-Grandpa Tunis,
but I couldn't touch them or talk to them. It wasn't like with
Nathaniel. "He wants me to solve his murder," I go on. "But I
was wondering if you could . . . help."

Charlotte pauses. "I can't, really," she says. "That would
be like major interference where I don't belong. Like, if you
had a fight with your mother, and I stuck my nose into it.
Not good."

A shocking thought strikes me like a hammer: "Do you
know who killed him?" I demand. "If you knew who murdered

Nathaniel, would you tell me?" Suddenly I suck in my breath, and a cold sweat beads across my brow. "You're in touch with him, with the murderer's spirit, aren't you?"

There's silence on her end, or rather a sound like she's clicking a ballpoint pen open, closed, nervously. Finally, Charlotte says, "Trust me, I'm on your side, Lori, but there's a natural order to the universe, and it's not my destiny to shake it up. *You* absolutely must find the answer for Nathaniel Pierce. You, not me."

20

AS SOON AS I hang up with Charlotte, I leave the house again. I'm pulled by forces I do not understand — a compulsion that demands that I get to Nathaniel's grave *now*. I find myself running toward the Evergreen gatehouse. There's a stitch in my side, and my mind's a fury of questions. Edison Larch, Henry Baldwin, the Lincoln ring. Everything is so fuzzy, and just when I think I grasp something, it's a handful of air.

Can I keep Nathaniel here if I *don't* solve the murder? Charlotte says he disappears after the Battle Days end. But maybe if I tell him I have a lead on the mystery, he can hang on . . . forever. I want to keep him with me, I realize. Selfishly.

But deep in the center of my being I know that if I don't solve his mystery, he'll simply fade away and suffer until someone else comes along. I can't bear that. I'm the one, he says. I have to do it, and somehow I sense there's a clue that will be revealed to me at his grave.

Inside the entrance to Evergreen Cemetery stands the gray-black statue of Elizabeth Thorn that I noticed the night of the ghost tour. In the daylight, I see her clearly. She holds the back of her wrist to her brow, and her fingers look gnarled with age and work. Her eyes are downcast, her face drawn and weary, her hair in an untidy bun at her neck. A shovel and some other long-handled tool lean against her flowing dress. Gravedigger's tools. She looks hot, defeated, depressed, totally exhausted, and pregnant.

I look up into her face. I *know* this woman, this keeper of the cemetery, know her in ways I've never known a living soul.

Is her ghost here? I wonder. *Is she another spirit that can reach me?*

I try reaching out to her. *What can you tell me?* I think, studying the statue. There's no response. Well, did I really expect one? Still, somehow I sense what she means for me to know. I follow the trajectory of her work-worn fingers resting on the bridge of her nose, sure that she's pointing to Nathaniel's grave.

No! I'm way too practical to believe such an impossible thing. It's just that I don't know how to find his grave again. I came upon it accidentally in the dark the night of the ghost tour. Accidentally? Maybe I was actually guided there.

I turn reluctantly away from the Elizabeth Thorn statue and head over to the Evergreen office. The man behind the desk smiles like a typical undertaker when I ask him for Nathaniel's burial records. He slides the mouse to wake up his computer and he types in: *NATHANIEL PIERCE/PENNSYLVANIA/1863.*

There he is. I let out a small gasp, then clamp my hand to my mouth.

"Find your person?" the man asks, showing me a guide to the grave markers.

I don't bother answering. Outside, I dodge other people looking at the tombstones and head right to where Elizabeth Thorn is pointing. I couldn't stop if I wanted to, streaking irresistibly past dozens of graves until I get to the right one:

NATHANIEL HEMPSTEAD PIERCE

1844–1863

I've clenched my fists so hard that my nails are digging into my palms, but one hand juts out against my will. This marker seems older than the three clumped next to it. Those are merely warmed by the sun. This stone feels like a sizzling coal, so hot I can only touch it for a millisecond without burning my fingers. Just like the night of the ghost tour. With faith that the stone won't scorch me, I reach out, stunned to feel it cooling under my hand, as though the granite were alive for a few seconds and only now can return to bloodless stone.

On the grass in front of the marker, I sit with my legs tucked under me. No one's nearby, so I know it's safe to speak. I lower my voice and ask the marker, ask *him*, "What's the connection between the clues we have, Nathaniel? Are you hiding a detail about Edison Larch? Is there something else, someone else, that I'm missing all together? Talk to me. I'm here to listen. *Nathaniel, I need you right now, right here.*"

I get only silence from the grave, a silence so profound and exquisite that I can hear insects and worms in the earth and grass. I wait, holding my breath, as an elderly couple walks toward me and lays a wreath on a nearby grave. It's the Crandalls, I realize, who seem to show up wherever I am. Are they following me? I crane my neck trying to see the name of their dead person, but it's just out of my line of vision. Mr.

Crandall tips his golf cap in my direction, and Mrs. Crandall smiles, but I notice that she strains to catch the name on the gravestone I'm facing. She picks up a rock from a small pile nearby and lays it on Nathaniel's headstone.

"It's a custom among some cultures," she explains, "so the departed will know they've been visited and their spirits can rest in peace."

Soon they move on, and I watch them pause at the Elizabeth Thorn statue, then walk out of the cemetery. They're holding hands, but Mr. Crandall's about three steps ahead of Mrs. Crandall, who turns around and waves to me.

It's quiet now, and I'm alone, waiting, waiting for him, until the shadows grow long, and still he doesn't come.

Once night falls, I return to the inn, feeling let down by Nathaniel. Why didn't he show up at the graveyard? Deep in thought, I'm on my way upstairs, hoping none of the guests will corral me for fresh towels or toilet paper.

In the second-floor hall, Bertha and Amelia Wilhoit are standing head-to-head, like they're in a pitcher/catcher huddle. All I hear are the *swish-swish* of whispers, but as soon as I approach, Bertha jumps back, cradling a basket of Crabtree & Evelyn soaps, and says, extra loud for my benefit, "Well, if it isn't the famous novel-writer lady. You look a little frazzled, Ms. Wilhoit, if you don't mind my saying so."

Wilhoit's wearing an oversized olive-green tunic and black leggings. Her bottle-blond hair is headbanded into submission. And style queen that she is, she's in red stiletto backless heels.

Bertha says, "I hope your accommodations are up to snuff, because General Stuart is the finest room we have to offer, if you like southern warmongers."

"The room's quite satisfactory, Mrs. Dryden." Amelia shifts her eyes from me to Bertha. Why are they pretending they weren't speaking just now? There's something weird going on. Whatever it is makes me extra suspicious.

Bertha mutters something about chores downstairs and takes off in a hurry.

"Miss Chase," Wilhoit says, turning to me, "my room needs freshening. Clean sheets, a bit of Ajax swirled around the sink. Would you mind?"

The last thing I want to do right now is clean around the dozens of bottles of *product* in her bathroom, but I'm caught, and Charlotte's not around. I nod halfheartedly.

"I'll go out for a stroll while some chapters print, but please don't take too long. I must return to my work; deadlines loom," Ms. Wilhoit says, tottering away in those ridiculous heels.

I sigh. I know about deadlines looming. Tomorrow Nathaniel will disappear from my life.

Her room is messy — historical textbooks on Gettysburg are piled everywhere. On her desk is a framed photo of a rugged-looking, not very attractive man who seems a little familiar. Does Wilhoit have a boyfriend? Interesting.

I whip through the bathroom and have started to strip the bed when my cell phone rings in my pocket. The cheerful ring-tone is barely loud enough to hear over the clackety sound of Amelia Wilhoit's printer churning out page after page.

It's been a long time since I've had an actual phone call. The number's unfamiliar, but I answer and am ecstatic to find that it's Jocelyn.

"I'm so glad to talk to you," I say, leaving the bed as is and sinking into the overstuffed chair in the corner.

"I know," Jocelyn groans. "I miss you. We're out in Nowheresville. It's great for horses. People? Not so much. Internet zones in and out. I'm calling you from a pay phone now! The horsey girls are at dinner. Gotta make it quick, though, because I fed all the change in my pocket down the throat of this phone. What's up? How was that Scarlett O'Hara dance thingie last night?"

Wilhoit's printer stops, spitting papers all over the room and flashing a paper-jam message. Not my problem.

"Surreal. Everybody trussed up in vintage Civil War clothes, waltzing around like it's a hundred and fifty years ago all over again, except for the high-tech sound system pounding out the band's music." Should I tell her about seeing all the ghostly dancers? Not yet, not on the phone. "The guy I went with —"

"The live one, not the dead one."

I pause, a little irritated that she'd dismiss Nathaniel so easily.

"You there?"

"Yeah, just thinking how to tell you about this. Evan, the lawn-mower guy, he was oh-so-dashing in his Confederate uniform and really sweet, and I was having a great time, but then the real Civil War soldier, Nathaniel, showed up."

"Get out of here! The ghost? Did they fight over you? Blood and guts right there on the dance floor?"

"No, but once Nathaniel was there, it spoiled the whole evening, because he's the guy I really wanted to be with. It's just that he has that big problem."

"Which is that he's dead."

"Well, yes. And also the fact that he didn't die from the war — he was murdered, and I'm trying to figure out who did it before he disappears tomorrow at midnight."

Long whistle from Jos on the other end. "You're trying to

solve a murder that happened about a hundred and fifty years ago by tomorrow night? Yikes. How are you going to do that?"

It sounds ridiculous when she puts it that way, but all I can do is try. I wonder if Jocelyn actually believes me about Nathaniel, the way Evan seemed to. The way Charlotte does. Jos always thought our séance games were fun, nothing more.

I decide to change the subject. "How are *you*?" I ask.

Jocelyn sighs. "Sad news from the Poconos pastures. It's all over with Jude."

"Jude?" I say, confused, and then I remember — her sort-of summer boyfriend. I feel like a bad friend for not keeping her love life in mind. I've been sort of distracted with my own. "What happened?" I ask.

"He's into some other counselor now. Turns out his style is a different girl each week. He's more loyal to the horses."

"I'm sorry, Jos." I feel a lump in my throat as I think of Nathaniel. He might be loyal to me, but I can't keep him here, with me.

"Uh-oh, here come the prepubescent troops. Dinner's over. Girls! Girls!" Jocelyn shouts. "Stay right there a sec 'til I finish my call. Lori? It sounds like you need help. Should I come back next week? I can tell the camp my father's getting married this time. Maybe you'll be able to introduce me to Nathaniel?"

"Won't work. After July third he won't be around, whether I solve the murder or not. He can only materialize around the Battle Days."

"I didn't realize there were so many rules related to ghosts!" Jocelyn says, kind of teasing, but not. She can tell I'm upset. "Okay, I should go, but let's talk soon. Keep me posted! Ciao." And she hangs up, leaving me totally depressed as I face the truth: Nathaniel will leave me by midnight tomorrow, and I've made no headway on the murder.

I stand up from the chair, turn around, and realize Wilhoit's standing at the open door. "You're not done yet?" She's picking up pages strewn all over the floor. I hurry over to her bed. If I quickly plump the pillows, maybe she won't realize that I didn't change the sheets.

"How long can it take to make one bed?" she asks, scowling. "You might be more efficient if you weren't on the phone yakking about your social entanglements."

I freeze. Did Amelia Wilhoit overhear the whole conversation?

21

I SLEPT BADLY last night, worrying about Amelia Wilhoit and thinking about Nathaniel's grave. Early this morning, I leave Gertie sleeping at the foot of my bed and slip out of the house without seeing my parents or Bertha.

Down at the creek I feel that thickening of air again, and my heart skips a beat.

"Is this a good time?" the deep voice in my ear asks jauntily. "I'm trying to abide by your unreasonable rules."

"Yes, it is," I say, relieved, and I turn to see him, materialized and real in his blue uniform.

He greets me with a long kiss. I want to enjoy it even more than I already do, but my mind is elsewhere. I pull back.

"I went to your grave yesterday," I say. "And I asked for your help. But you didn't come."

"I am sorry," Nathaniel tells me somberly. "I wish I could have. Unfortunately it is very difficult for me to manifest at times." He reaches for my hand and I take it.

"Today is our last day," I whisper, feeling immeasurably sad.

We walk hand in hand, talking in low, intimate tones. It feels so normal. It isn't.

"If I could stay with you," Nathaniel says, "I would take you to Titusville to meet my mother and father." He bursts out laughing. I've never heard him laugh so hard like that. Somehow it makes him more human, more real, more losable, and I'm already starting to miss him.

"What's so funny?"

"Just imagining what they'd think of you dressed in short trousers and a shirt that leaves your arms and neck and shoulders open to the eye."

"It's the way people dress today!"

"I know, yes. It's just that you'd shock those old Pierces of Titusville. They're right proper folks."

I'm confused. "Do you — still see your parents?"

"You don't leave people you've loved behind, like a snake shedding its skin. They're wanting to know how all this turns out. I can feel them hovering near sometimes, but they're quiet, just waiting."

"And listening? Watching?" I think of him kissing me. What would his nineteenth-century parents think of our kissing right out in the open?

"No, just waiting for me to tell them everything's all right." He steps to the side and looks me over carefully. "Women in my day covered up neck to ankle. Some changes are better, like your talking machine that gives you information faster than an eye blink. Wish I could live in the present, to stay with you." He smiles, squeezes my hand, and adds, "I love the way you look, dressed so bold. I love you entirely, Lorelei Cordelia."

My heart soars at the sound of these words, and my own spill out unexpectedly: "I love you, too, Nathaniel Pierce. I do; I really do."

I've never said that to a boy before. How easy it is to say it when you mean it. Nathaniel squeezes my hands and beams at me and I stand on tiptoe to kiss him.

• • •

But we're no closer to solving the murder.

My phone rings. I reach into the back pocket of my shorts and pull it out. Evan's calling. What great timing.

"Hi, I can't talk to you right now," I say into the phone, noticing Nathaniel's quizzical look.

"Not much of a greeting for the guy who's about to make your day."

"Can you text me about it?" I'm afraid Nathaniel will get impatient and vanish again.

"Another talking machine?" Nathaniel says. "In the words of the Bard, 'O brave new world.'"

That's in one ear. In my other ear Evan's saying, "I'll make it quick. I've been doing some Internet research. Followed a few dead leads, but I hit on a live one, and boy is it good. Google 'Dryden Bluefin Harbor Maine.' Call me when you're done — we've got some dicey stuff to discuss." *Click.*

I give a deep sigh, tucking my phone back in my pocket. Nathaniel is frowning at me. The last thing I want to do now is leave him, especially after what we've just said to each other. But I need to follow up on Evan's research while it's still fresh in my mind.

"I'm sorry," I tell Nathaniel, "but there's something I have to take care of right away. It might have something to do with your murder, but I can't say how, yet. Can we meet again later? I might have something important to tell you."

He sounds irritated. "Let's meet at Devil's Den."

"What's that — a tavern? A shop?"

"It's a battlefield where many of us fell. You'll find it on a Gettysburg map. Wait for me. I'll be there. We haven't much time."

The sun is high in the sky, half blinding me. Someone's coming toward us, a woman. Only one person would be walking on a country road in needle-thin heels. Amelia Wilhoit. Oh, man, why can't she be up in her room like she usually is, pecking away at her laptop?

"Someone from the house is coming," I whisper to Nathaniel. "You'd better make yourself scarce, quick." Wilhoit wouldn't see him anyway, but still I'm nervous having him around, especially since she heard me talking about him to Jocelyn last night. Nathaniel nods, and the air around me changes until I know he's gone. Where does he go when he's not with me?

"Hello, Ms. Wilhoit!" I'm trying to chirp like Mom does, but I come off sounding like a demented parakeet.

She stops abruptly, hands clasped across her chest. "You gave me such a start."

I don't believe her act. She slides her squinty eyes from me to the empty space beside me, like she's looking for someone. "Are you alone? I thought I heard you talking to someone." Her husky voice turns hard. "Was it that murdered soldier you were having a nice afternoon stroll with, cozy as two cooing doves?"

I swallow. Did she really see Nathaniel, or is she just throwing my own words back at me? "You must be mistaken. I was just on the phone."

"Maybe so, but I know about that bedraggled Union soldier, the one who met an unfortunate early demise. You, my friend, must be more careful about what you say on the phone. You never know who's listening." I'm fuming, but I hold my tongue as she adds, "Your parents would find this relationship rather startling, would you agree?"

And with that she turns tail and walks quickly toward the house, those stupid stiletto heels digging into the soft dirt of the road like cleats and leaving me feeling like I'm about to be blackmailed. But why?

Back in my room, I take out my laptop and, as Evan instructed, type in "Dryden Bluefin Harbor Maine." The first link is to an article in the archives of the weekly *Bluefin Harbor Trumpet*, from last year. I read:

Mrs. Livingston Langmor of Bluefin Harbor reported the mysterious disappearance of the pocket watch and fob belonging to the late Mr. Langmor. It was a gift to his grandfather from President Rutherford Hayes. "It's quite precious, though its sentimental significance far exceeds its monetary value," Mrs. Langmor told this reporter. Questioned in connection with the loss of this piece of historical memorabilia was Mrs. Langmor's housekeeper, Bertha Dryden. She and her gardener husband, Joseph Dryden, joined the household staff late last year. Bertha Dryden said, "Mrs. Langmor, poor dear, misplaces her cane, her glasses, and her hearing aids several times a day. You'll see; the watch will turn up in a day or two." The Bluefin Harbor sheriff's department continues to investigate. Expect an update in next Thursday's issue of The Trumpet.

I pore over the article twice. Sure sounds like the Drydens aren't on the up-and-up. Now I'm convinced that they're after something hidden here at Coolspring Inn. And the pocket watch was a presidential artifact. It reminds me of the Lincoln ring.

So I Google "Death of William Lincoln" on a whim. There's a lot of general information, none of which seems to trigger a brilliant insight. I keep skimming through more and more sites until — whoa! — something practically lights up in neon on my screen. At William Lincoln's death, the attending doctor's name was Richard V. Anderson.

Initials: RVA. Like on the amputation kit.

My thoughts race. Could that be Nathaniel's doc — the man who had the ring? Which might have actually been Abraham Lincoln's baby ring. Which would be incredibly valuable today. Which went missing. Which is maybe what the Drydens are searching for. Which might be somehow connected to Nathaniel's murder.

My breath's coming in pants, like Gertie's. I'm hyped with excitement, sure that the ring's hidden in the RVA box, and that's why Old Dryden was hunting for it. Nathaniel said that his friend Wince probably went to the hospital and hid the ring among the doctor's personal possessions. What could be more personal than your very own handy-dandy amputation kit?

"Off the bed, Gertie Girl, and no telling anyone what you see, agreed?" She couldn't care less, because a cricket's leading her on a merry chase.

The RVA kit is still hidden inside my pillow. The hinges

are fragile, rusted with age, so I open the box carefully and
notice that faint words are engraved on the inside of the lid:

IN TIME AND WITH WATER,

EVERYTHING CHANGES

Leonardo da Vinci

What's that got to do with bloody limbs? I pull out the
small drawer, lift out each surgical knife, and lay them all on
the floor. The small knives are so light they could be letter
openers. Some have hooks, like dental hygienists use to clean
your teeth. Some fold like jackknives. They all look menacing.
What were they used for, exactly? Cutting into skin? Severing
blood vessels or nerves? I'm chilled to the core, and I hug
myself, shuddering.

I search the inside of the entire box to the edges, to see if
the ring is in there somewhere, but have no luck. I pick up the
handsaw, which has greater heft than the other tools. The handle's made of elephant ivory, and it's warm to the touch. A
familiar scent wafts up from the velvet lining. Chloroform.
Bertha said Civil War doctors used it as an anesthetic, the rare
times they had any. They covered the soldier's nose and mouth
with a towel dipped in the chloroform. Did that free the patient

from pain, or terrify him because he couldn't breathe or cry out? And how many soldiers died from inhaling too much of the drug?

A thumb flick across the blade of the handsaw jangles my nerves. The blade must have been sharp long ago, but now it's dulled by the hundreds of bones it must have sliced through. Trying to picture Dr. Anderson, I wonder how it felt to him to cut off a man's arm or leg.

The handle of the handsaw has tiny freckle-sized screws in it, just begging me to loosen them and see how the saw's constructed and what's hidden inside. I've always been interested in putting things together and taking them apart. Maybe that's why I'm drawn to Nathaniel's mystery.

"I'll be right back, Gertie," I promise.

In the kitchen, Dad's on his knees, his head in the gaping cave where a drawer once fit. "Oh, Lorelei." He mutters, "There's no end to the things that don't work in this place. This drawer swelled in the humidity and wouldn't slide open."

I want to say *I told you not to buy this place*, but of course, if he hadn't, I wouldn't have met Nathaniel.

"Mind if I look for a small screwdriver?" I ask him. I rummage around in the toolbox at his feet. "I need the tiniest one, the kind you'd use to fix the screws on eyeglasses."

"Right-hand corner. You'll see a small kit in a plastic tube."

"Thanks. I'll bring it back next time I climb down from the tower."

Upstairs, Gertie yaps as my door creaks open. "It's me. Remember me?" I say, coming back inside and sitting down on the floor beside the box.

One by one the four screws in the ivory handle of the saw come loose. The ivory lifts off with just the slightest prying of the small screwdriver. I'm sure the ring's in there.

But there's nothing inside. Another dead end.

22

ALL THE FAKE-GENUINE Battle reenactments in the area are over. All's quiet on the field.

Later that day, I find myself propped up between huge granite rocks in a narrow cutout called Devil's Den.

I looked at a battlefield map, as Nathaniel recommended. Union sharpshooters crouched in Devil's Den on the second day of the Battle. Across from here is Little Round Top, another intense Battle site, and between Little Round Top and where I am lies the Valley of Death. Sounds like the ideal spot to meet a ghost. It's also secluded, meaning no one will see or hear

Nathaniel. Most people are smart enough, or chicken enough, to obey the signs that say no climbing on the rocks. Not me. A shadowy basement — that's another story, but a few gigantic, jagged, slippery boulders aren't going to spook me.

Dropping down into the cutout is easy. Waiting isn't. Ten, fifteen minutes drag by. I'm drowsing in that weird dream space where you hear the grass in the breeze and the bugs scuttling under your feet, but you wouldn't budge if a battalion of them marched across you. Asleep, but not quite. There's a low rumble of a howl, like a distant animal baying at the moon, or a lonesome train whistle at night. And then it's a chorus of quiet voices, no words distinct. A dozen voices, a thousand, ten thousand. The sounds take shape, like a photograph developing. They're coming from the rocks, the singing rocks. . . .

See this gets to Liza Lou down home in . . . I'm not gonna make it, Cap'n . . . Leave me be, get the horse, ain't fair to the horse, it ain't her war . . . Pretty soon I'ma feel nothin' but sweet serenity . . . Swing low, sweet chariot, comin' for to carry me home . . .

I know these are the dead of Gettysburg, the spirits that have no peace. I lie down in the brush, in the narrow canyon between the boulders. The rocks around me thrum with sound. The voices wash over me, pump through me like my own blood.

Where ya hurt, soldier . . . All's I want is a bite of Ma's rabbit stew once more . . . Sun beating down . . . Glory be, it's lonely out

here all alone . . . Stories to tell my daughters if'n I make it back to
Memphis . . . I done run away, suh, to fight wid you . . .

I should be scared, wondering if I'm hallucinating. I'm not.
These voices are a comforting choir. Each comes with a fleeting picture of a soldier in this valley. White, brown, northern,
southern, wounded, able-bodied. And the women, children, and
old folks waiting for them at home. I wonder if I'm among them,
if I'm dead, and that's why Nathaniel is so real to me. Nathaniel,
who is now swinging his legs over a boulder and dropping
down into the spot next to me.

The voices fade away as though they were a warm-up act
for the main attraction. I rouse myself from the stupor, reluctant to let go of all those thousands of others. But here is
Nathaniel, and I'm *not* dead. I am pulsing with life.

"It took you long enough to get here," I murmur.

"I came a long way," he says with a sweet, teasing smile.
And doesn't *that* raise a few questions that we don't have time to
explore right now? I'm snapping to attention.

"It's okay. I wasn't alone."

"I know," Nathaniel says. What part did he have in sharing
those haunting, comforting voices with me? He finds a spot
against gray rock, just wide enough for our shoulders to nest in.
His lips on mine are so alive, warm, and eager. I turn my face

up to him for more kisses, until I can barely breathe. I'd gladly stay here, eyes closed, tasting the sweet fruit of his lips. Forever.

But we need to talk. So I pull away, angling my body to face him, my body that's silently ticking like a clock from the nearness of him. He reads the urgency in my face, so he straightens up.

"Let's start pulling clues together, Nathaniel," I say. "What's the connection between the Drydens, who are on staff at my house; Winston Carmody, who built my house; your doctor, who I now know is named Anderson —"

"Yes, now that you say it." Nathaniel nods, squinting at the memory. "Doc Anderson — Robert, I believe."

"Richard. Plus Lincoln's ring, and Edison Larch. How are they connected?"

"I don't know the Drydens . . ." he starts to say, but because I'm anxious about the time slipping away, I interrupt him.

"I found out that Bertha and Joseph Dryden were questioned about a recent theft in Maine, a pocket watch that once belonged to President Rutherford Hayes. Does that raise any flags for you?"

"Flags? Union, or Confederate?"

"I mean, does it remind you of anything, such as the ring that belonged to the Lincoln family?" I fill him in about Old

Dryden in my cellar, Doctor Anderson's amputation kit, and even my nagging suspicion that Amelia Wilhoit and Bertha are in cahoots, which is an unknown word, but he figures out the meaning.

"You think the Drydens are looking for Lincoln's ring? I can't see how it relates to Edison and Wince, or to the man who shot me."

"Me neither," I admit, "but it's there, somewhere. I feel like the ring is the key to the whole thing, but for the life of me, I can't figure it out."

"For the life of you . . . for the death of me. That puts it all in balance."

My watch says five thirty. "I've got to get home for dinner, or Mom will send the vigilantes after me. I don't know how this works, Nathaniel, but can you sort of listen for me, in case I need you to come? I'll meet you out by the creek. We have a lot of work to do before midnight."

"If you concentrate deeply, you can communicate with me across time and space, but I'll stay near the creek, I promise. Now, let me get you home like a proper gentleman."

"My parents —"

"Don't fret; they won't see me."

• • •

Gertie sitting on my feet is the only thing that keeps me from escaping during dinner. We're eating Chinese takeout in the kitchen, dipping our chopsticks into the cartons. Mom would never have allowed such primitive behavior back in Philadelphia.

"I cannot believe we're doing this," Mom says, popping a soggy leaf of bok choy into her mouth.

"You know, Miriam, people eat from communal bowls in most of the developing world."

"Yes, Vernon, but we used to be developed," Mom says, smacking her lips.

Gertie has no interest in snow peas, so she's happily dozing under the table, holding out for more hearty grub; the kind that's poured out of a twenty-pound bag.

"Are we done?" I ask.

"What's your hurry, Lorelei?" Dad asks.

"Only three hours of daylight left."

"So? Where do you need to be?" asks Mom.

"Nowhere." I fidget. "It's just that it's the last Battle Day, and people will be checking out tomorrow, and we've got to turn the rooms around for new guests, and then all the Harleys will be here for Biker Week."

"Next week, honey. Tonight's a breather," Mom says.

"I need to check my e-mail."

Mom sighs. "All right, go."

On my way to the stairs, I pass the giant map posted on the wall by the front entrance. All the guests study it when they check in, and then they get a welcome packet with a copy of it showing the position of our land in relation to the major battles. The wall map's captioned in an old-fashioned font:

Coolspring, 1860

Something looks funny about it to me when I see it this time, and I do a double take. I grab one of the eight-by-ten copies of the map and take it back to my room to study, to figure out what's giving me such a nagging feeling.

Amelia Wilhoit passes Gertie and me on the stairs. She's got a smug look on her face. "Where are your parents?"

"Out for a walk." Not sure why I'm lying to her. Well, yeah, I do know why.

"Perhaps I'll run into them."

I hope not.

My laptop cursor's winking as I open my e-mail. What's so important that someone sent me six messages in an hour? The most recent one says:

lawnboy@quagmire.net
why aren't you answering????? thought

you'd be chomping to call me after you
googled the drydens

I *do* want to talk to him about that, but this map's calling for my attention right now. I look at the paper. There were a lot more trees then. Some had to be cut down to clear space for the house. Orienting myself to the north/south position, I see the original house at the top of a small hill.

I mentally sketch in the current house, larger than the one that burned down a century ago. I picture myself looking out my high window in the 1860s, sweating like a goat in one of those miserably hot dresses, tight at the neck and skimming my lace-up boots. In my daydream, old-fashioned Lori — Lorelei Cordelia — gazes down toward the creek and the row of trees on the other side of it.

Wait. There's no creek on the map. What? I blink at the paper, and double-check the east/west orientation. Here's the front of the house, here's the hill leading down to the creek. Where's the creek? My eyes travel to the space where the shed will be built. There's something there on the map darker than the rest of the drawing. Water? I lean closer, squinting, and I can just make out the faint words: *Coolspring Pond.*

What's a pond, anyway? A small lake? A round creek? A fat stream? A babbling brook? Googling *pond* only confuses the questions. Evan does landscaping — maybe he would know. I give him a call.

"Lori Chase? Phoning me? Call the TV stations!" Evan answers. "Sorry for the sarcasm. Talk to me."

"It's about ponds and creeks."

"This ought to be a stimulating conversation," Evan says, laughing.

"It could be, if you've got an answer to the latest weird development in my life. I'm studying that map of the grounds from 1860. You know the creek? It's not on the map. Instead there's something called Coolspring Pond, and it's where the shed stands today. The shed, obviously, isn't underwater. Do you know why?"

"Very observant, Ms. Chase. I can help you with this one. A pond does this thing called succession, meaning that over time — I'm talking centuries or it could be just decades, plant life on the bottom — do I hear you yawning in boredom?"

"I'm tingling with excitement."

"Right, so the bottom of the pond builds up and, abra-cadabra, the pond changes into a landform, like a meadow or grassland. The pond disappears. And over time, rainwater or springwater forms a new pond in a low point of the area. Such as the creek."

"So, you're telling me that Coolspring Creek is new?"

"Relatively. Maybe a hundred years."

"And the original 1860s pond is now grassland?"

"Ain't nature grand? Anything else on your mind? Such as a movie this weekend?"

"I'll get back to you on that. Gotta go now."

"Yeah, that dead guy is waiting for you," Evan says, with a slight edge. "See ya."

I hang up and keep staring at the map. Okay, so what does all this mean? Absolutely nothing to me . . . yet. I have to find Nathaniel if I'm ever going to solve the mystery, and it has to be before midnight tonight. When we were talking before, Nathaniel tried to tell me why he can only stay in Gettysburg during the Battle Days. It's a promise he made to himself a hundred years before I was born. And so his physical being withers like autumn leaves by midnight, July third, and turns to the winter of his soul. That's the way he explained it.

I still don't understand. All I know is that after midnight tonight, he'll be gone, and I'll be left here without him. At least if I can solve the murder, I can send him off in peace. But it's awful, unfair, and horribly sad, and I won't get over it. Ever.

23

IT'S THAT TIME on a summer evening, sevenish, when the sun is bright and burnishing, and you think it can't possibly get dark, but it will. Time is sprinting away, and Evan's slowly crisscrossing the lawn on the riding mower, not that seven p.m. is the ideal time to mow, and not that it needs mowing. I'm sure he just wants to get near me, sitting down here by the creek, the *new* creek, but he's not sure how. He's been amazing to put up with my attitude and the fact that I'm mooning around over some other guy, a ghostly one at that. I start to think, *Get a life,*

Evan, but the truth is, he's funny and smart and helpful. I like him, and I sure need a friend right now.

Gertie follows the lawn mower and whips around the U-turns with Evan. Each time they pass me, a swath closer to the creek, Evan shouts out something — lines of a song or a famous quote. "She'll be comin' 'round the mountain when she comes. . . ." or "Quoth the raven, nevermore. . . ."

It's calculated to make me smile, and it works. I'm always on the verge of tears around Nathaniel, and I used to be a person who only cried at sappy movies. I once read that Victorian women caught their tears and stored them in small bottles. If I had one of those tear catchers, it would be overflowing with Nathaniel's contagious sweet sorrow and my grief over losing him by midnight.

Nathaniel and Evan are polar opposites. This guy on the riding mower is a hopeless optimist. He's like confetti, sprinkling me with colors, which makes me wonder: Am I happier when I'm miserable? That's sick. Or is that what love is supposed to feel like? Love and loss and love lost.

The next time Evan rides by ("We all live in a yellow submarine . . .") I wave him over, and he's quick to turn off the motor and join me on the bank of the creek. Gertie circles a spot between us and drops down for a nap. Our chaperone.

"Can I talk to you about the Edison factor?" I ask him.

"What, the dead-soldier mystery again?" Evan rolls his eyes, but then smiles at me. "It's all right. I'm a sucker for a spicy murder and a spunky girl detective." He leans forward, and without much warning plants his lips on mine.

I stagger back. "Hey, what're you doing?"

"It's called a kiss, that thing people do with their lips, remember?" He straightens up, flashing me questioning eyes: *Okay?*

"It's okay." In fact, it was pretty nice, considering that he's the second guy to kiss me today. Or this year. Jocelyn won't believe this when I tell her. I feel a flash of guilt when I think of Nathaniel. Is he somewhere nearby? Did he see Evan kiss me?

"So, what about the Edison factor?" Evan asks, bringing me back to earth.

I shake my head, trying not to blush or dwell too much on our quick kiss. It's funny how things *don't* feel awkward.

"I'm wondering," I say, "if the evidence is persuasive enough to tell Nathaniel that Edison's the one who shot him. He doesn't want to believe a friend could do such a thing. But I have to tell him tonight. Tomorrow's too late."

Evan shrugs. "The guy's waited, what? A hundred and fifty years already? He's got eternity stretched out ahead of him like an endless lawn that always needs mowing. What's the big rush?"

"It's just something I need to do. I don't get it myself, but I know he'll be gone by midnight," I tell Evan, feeling my brow and nose wrinkle in a way that would make Mom say, *Loosen up, honey. You'll get creases before you know it.*

Evan's face is down-turned in an exaggerated frown. "You can do it. You do difficult stuff in tricky situations all the time, right, catcher? Batter hits a pop-up, you gotta toss off your mask and sprint to the infield to catch it, toss it to first."

"You play softball? Baseball?" I ask hopefully, then remember his pathetic fumbles.

"Nah, but you do. I watched a YouTube video of your team from last summer, Liberty Bells vs. Wranglers." I'm surprised and a little flattered. He grins. "So, let's say there are a bunch of murder suspects warming up in the bullpen. It's the bottom of the seventh, two outs, score's three to two, your team. The dead guy's covering first base. Edison saunters up to the plate, swinging his mighty bat. Pitcher throws a yakker, Edison bunts. Woohoo, it's all up to you to nail it. Mask flies off into the dirt, you seize the ball and fling it to first. Thud, right in the dead guy's glove. He tags Edison just to be sure. Game over. Your team slides by in a squeaker."

"That was amazing, Evan!"

"Yeah, I've been getting the lingo down to impress you." His eyes crinkle as he grins. "Now let's take a dip," he adds. "I think better underwater."

The water does look enticing, and I'd really like to let it roll over me, especially in this steamy heat. We both kick off our shoes and slide down the bank. The creek's only three feet deep, but squatting gives us plenty of cool water up to our necks. My T-shirt balloons around me. It's only now, with my wet hair slapping the back of my shirt, that I realize how tense I've been, every muscle knotted. The weight of water on my chest begins to relax me until I lean back and float, squinting at the sun slowly fading in the whipped-cream clouds drifting by. Evan and I, we're floating side by side so peacefully, our fingers barely touching, even though my mind is racing, sifting through the names and facts and guesses that plague me.

"Come on in, Gertie," Evan calls, and Gertie makes a giant splash in her dive. What an attention grabber. She swims to the center of the creek and suddenly begins whimpering, just as she did the other time we were out here.

"What is it, Gertie Girl?" I ask. Evan and I both tilt to our feet and walk across the sandy bottom of the creek. Gertie's going nuts, growling and whimpering and pawing the water. Fear heightens the blue rings of her eyes. "What is it?" I ask, now glancing at Evan. "Is there a sandbar? A sudden drop?"

I think of something I heard on the ghost tour about Weinbrenner Creek — that there were wounded soldiers who drowned in the flash flood of July fourth. My heart pounds. Is there a body under the water? Then I remember that this creek didn't even exist in 1863. But there could have been a soldier buried here when it was dry land. Nathaniel told me about the shallow graves and makeshift markers of dead wood.

Before I can warn Evan about the grisly thing he's about to find, he goes under where Gertie's frantically treading water, pokes his head out for a deep breath, then dives back down. Gertie scuttles to the bank, panting and barking and shaking water in a wide, splashy arc. I can't bring myself to duck under and encounter what might be there.

Evan comes up with a curious look on his face.

"What? What's down there?" I ask anxiously.

"Just this," he says, placing something in my hand. It's slick and slimy, too large for my fingers to fold around, but it fills my palm. It feels scummy, like a wad you'd find stuck in a kitchen pipe, and my first impulse is to toss it back in the water, until Evan says, "Whatever this is, it sure spooked Gertie. Look at her over there."

We both surface and slog over wet sand, up the bank to where Gertie's pacing. One look at the thing in my hand, dripping water and slime between my fingers, and she backs off and yowls in a way I've never heard before.

Our clothes cling to us. We're shivering despite the lingering sun.

"What do you think this is?" Evan asks, touching the square package in my hand. It's wrapped in something rubbery, sealed tight. My fingers can't pry it open.

"Where did you find it, exactly?"

"Floating in a pile of decayed leaves, anchored by silt. It was probably buried in the ground a long time ago, but as the silt built up and the creek eroded the ground as it formed, this thing came to the surface. That's my semiprofessional, as-yet-uneducated opinion. Open it."

"I can't. It's sealed watertight, but it's real squishy and disgusting."

"I have a Swiss Army knife in my pocket, if it hasn't floated away." Water slurgs out of his clothes as he stretches to retrieve the knife. Gertie is way up the hill, crouching in the bushes in front of the house. Evan cuts through the black, rubbery stuff, and it opens like a flower in my palm. Inside's a teakwood box about two inches square. The size of a ring box. Excitement bursts like fireworks deep within me; I can hardly catch my breath.

The ring.

This is *it*!

Evan's knife pries the ring box open. There's a large piece of paper folded and refolded into a square to fit in the box. I peek under the paper and see a small green bag. I open it and out falls a ring. A tiny, beautiful gold ring. *The* ring — Abraham Lincoln's son's ring. It must be!

"Oh, wow," Evan breathes.

My hands are trembling. Quickly, I stash the ring back in the bag. I have a sense I need to protect it.

"What's that piece of paper?" Evan asks, pointing. "Can you unfold it?"

"Wait a sec," I say. "You got a towel up there on the mower? I need to make sure my hands are totally dry, because if I'm right, the paper is more than a hundred years old."

24

EVAN BRINGS ME the towel, Gertie following tentatively behind him. She seems okay now that we've got the box open. They both sit beside me on the bank and peer over my shoulder as I carefully unfold the paper, which is old-fashioned onionskin, brittle with age. It opens to sixty-four squares like small windowpanes. I skim the first few words, printed in a small, tight hand, to get the gist of it, and I'm reeling with astonishment.

"What?" Evan asks. "Read it out loud."

"I have to read it to myself first."

"I give you two minutes," Evan warns, "and then I'm snapping it out of your hands."

I read:

MAY IT BE UNDERSTOOD THAT THIS IS MY LAST CONFESSION. MY WORLDLY GOODS HAVE LONG AGO BEEN DISPERSED, BUT THE SPIRIT OF WHO I AM APPEARS HEREIN. YOU WHO ARE READING THIS, I PRAY YOU WILL GRANT ME DISPENSATION WHEN THE TRUTH UNFOLDS.

I REMAINED IN GETTYSBURG WHEN THE WAR ENDED, HAVING CAUGHT THE EYE OF VIENNA JOOST, A WOMAN OF UNCOMMON INTELLIGENCE AND INNER BEAUTY. AS A YOUNG DOCTOR, I BEGAN TO FASHION AND CONSTRUCT ARTIFICIAL LIMBS FOR THE SOLDIERS WHO LOST ARMS AND LEGS DURING THE ORDEAL OF BATTLE HERE. I FOLLOWED IN THE DEDICATED TRADITION OF DR. RICHARD ANDERSON, WHOM I ADMIRED. AFTER HIS UNTIMELY DEATH, I ACQUIRED HIS TRUSTED AMPUTATION KIT, WHICH I USED RARELY.

"Time's up. Who's it from?" Evan asks.

"Shh. Let me finish, and then you can read it." My thoughts are spinning. This is from someone who knew Nathaniel's doctor.

> I WAS PRESENT AT THE DEDICATION OF THE SOLDIERS' CEMETERY IN NOVEMBER OF 1863, AT WHICH PRESIDENT LINCOLN SPOKE BRIEFLY, YET SO ELOQUENTLY. THE ALMIGHTY KNOWS I SHOULD HAVE RETURNED MR. LINCOLN'S PROPERTY, HIS YOUNG SON'S RING, THEN, BUT I DID NOT. MY VIENNA WAS WITH CHILD, AND I FANCIED THAT RING UPON THE FINGER OF MY UNBORN SON.

"Oh no," I murmur.

"What? WHAT?" Evan looks worried, but I wave him away and continue reading silently.

> TO OUR UNREMITTING GRIEF, OUR INFANT SON PASSED TWO HOURS AFTER HIS BIRTH, WITH THE RING ON HIS TINY THUMB.

"Oh, that's so sad."

"Tell me it's not from Nathaniel himself. It's not, is it?"

I shake my head. "I think it's from his friend in the battle here. A man named Wince Carmody."

"Who built your house," Evan adds.

"Please let me finish."

> VIENNA WAS BEYOND SORROW AS OUR BABY WAS LOWERED INTO THE GROUND AT EVERGREEN CEMETERY, THROUGH THE GENEROUS SERVICES OF MRS. PETER THORN. ELIZABETH THORN WAS A DEAR FRIEND OF MY VIENNA'S, AND DEEPLY AGGRIEVED AT OUR SON'S DEMISE.

"Elizabeth Thorn," I murmur. "Now I know why I've been so obsessed by her statue at Evergreen."

Evan groans with impatience.

> I THOUGHT TO BURY THE RING WITH THE BOY, GOD PROTECT HIS ETERNAL SOUL, BUT I COULD NOT BRING MYSELF TO LET IT GO. THE RING IS CURIOUSLY BOTH A BLESSING AND A CURSE — A REMINDER OF A DEAR FRIEND AND OF MY SON'S BRIEF LIGHT SHINING IN THIS WORLD. THUS, IT IS HERE BURIED IN AN IMPERMEABLE BOX, DEEP IN THE HALLOWED GROUND OF A FIELD HOSPITAL.

MY PRAYER IS THAT NO OTHER FATHER OR
MOTHER WILL BE BLINDED BY ITS GLITTER AND
SUFFER THE LOSS OF A CHILD WHO WEARS IT.

I begin to read aloud, pulling Evan into the sad saga.

"'Any who remember me, or who happen upon this letter, please reckon that I have tried to be a kind man, a good doctor, and a loyal friend. I refer to my comrade in arms in the 93rd Pennsylvania Infantry, Nathaniel Pierce.

"'I was a party to his fatal wounding at the behest of another soldier, whose obsession was vengeance for something over which young Pierce had no control. The wrongdoer, even in the darkest crevice of his soul, professed to be a faithful friend as he pointed his pistol. God save us from such acts of friendship.'

"Yes!" I exclaim. "It *was* Edison Larch. I knew it. This is proof."

"Let me see." Evan slides the letter away from me and scans it as I read it again over his shoulder. His eyebrows rise when he comes to the part about the ring, but he doesn't comment until the paragraph about the *fatal wounding.* "This isn't proof at all, Lori. He doesn't mention Edison by name. It wouldn't stand up in court even in a TV script."

"Yes it would!" I insist, sinking back on my heels. Then Evan reads the next paragraph aloud:

"'On that fateful day, Pierce lay on a bed of pain in our tent. I had moved him to a sitting position, the better to swallow a mouthful of a therapeutic tea infusion. Clutching a pistol in both hands, Edison Larch crept up behind my friend. I let go of Pierce, who fell forward, unconscious. Larch and I tussled. We tumbled to the ground behind Pierce as I tried to wrestle the gun away. God help me, my fingers were on the trigger when the gun fired and Pierce gasped his final, labored breath.'"

"Wince did it? No!" I shout.

"It's right here, in his own handwriting," Evan affirms, and he continues reading aloud:

"'My life dwindles and I cannot go to the grave with this confession unvoiced. Vienna met her maker three years ago. We were never blessed with another child, and thus I am left without an heir. I bequeath, therefore, to the young of the world, a future of love, good work, and far more peace of mind than I have enjoyed in my lifetime.

"'Written this day, March 6, 1904. Gettysburg, Pennsylvania. Dr. Winston Jeremiah Carmody, Jr.'"

Then there's nothing we can say, Evan and I, so we sit in silence, shoulder to shoulder, but not touching, until he quietly leaves.

The mystery is solved, but I feel terrible. I have to break the news to Nathaniel tonight, before midnight. I put the letter back inside the box with the ring and make my way back toward the inn. Deep in thought about how I'm going to tell him, I almost stumble over Mr. Crandall's feet. Both the Crandalls are sprawled in Adirondack chairs halfway between the creek and the house. Mrs. Crandall is knitting something fuzzy and orange. Her husband is tapping out a rhythm on the arm of the chair.

"Hi-ho, Miss Lori," says Mr. Crandall. "We've been waiting for you."

I do *not* want to talk. I stuff the ring box in my soggy pocket. They see, but don't comment. I've got to get the ring and Wince's letter up to my room to hide them in my pillow with the RVA kit, but the Crandalls aren't letting me get away that easily.

"I believe we must chat, Miss Lori. The time has come," says Mr. Crandall.

His wife pats the wide arm of her chair for me to perch on. Reluctantly, I sit down and face Mr. Crandall, still dripping creek water.

"It is not by accident that Mother Crandall and I came to Coolspring Inn this week," he begins. "I believe we were called here. We quickly picked up on your potential, Miss Lori, and we're here to assist."

"Potential?" I keep getting an elbow to the ribs as the knitter works her way across an orange row, but she doesn't seem to notice me scooting farther and farther into the corner of the chair to avoid her elbow.

"Potential for communicating with people on the Other Side," she says sweetly. "The other side of the divide between this world of flesh, and the next world of spirit. Charlotte, of course, is an old hand, but you're fairly green at this, my dear, and we felt you needed a guide — a Sherpa, if you will."

It takes me a second to comprehend what the Crandalls are saying. So they see spirits, too? Then something dawns on me: "That's why you've been following me everywhere? And you're the ones who slipped the note under my door about seeing 'them.'"

"Oh, did that alarm you? Beg your forgiveness," says Mr. Crandall. "Just thought you should know that you were not alone in encountering the spirits. They're all around us."

"Think of it like the busiest street in New York City," explains Mrs. Crandall with a tinkly laugh. "People going hither and yon, sliding past one another on their personal doings."

I think of all the ghosts I saw at the ball with Evan and nod. "You make it sound so normal. Isn't it scary?"

"Well, yes, at first. But so is bungee jumping over a water-fall," Mr. Crandall booms. "What's the worst that could happen?"

I'm thinking, *The bungee cord could snap and you'd be plunged to your death onto craggy rocks in icy water, and if hypothermia didn't kill you, the jagged rocks would rip you to bits.*

Mrs. Crandall continues, "Most spirits just go about their daily chores and pay no attention to us. Some hover over us like rolling clouds to see how we're faring. They want us to do well; they truly do." I nod again, thinking of Nathaniel. "Others?" Mrs. Crandall sticks a needle into the ball of yarn and frowns.

"Which is why Mother and I are here at Coolspring Inn," Mr. Crandall chimes in. "Not all spirits are friendly. We sensed a malevolent spirit in this house."

"We may be right, and also wrong," Mrs. Crandall says with a faint smile. "It's entirely possible that the malevolent spirit isn't a spirit at all, and that there isn't only one. It might well be a whole bevy of living souls doing evil work."

"Be careful." Mr. Crandall's terse words strike fear in my heart.

"What if I don't want to do this, see and talk to spirits?" I blurt out. "What if it's just too hard?"

Mrs. Crandall nods. "Yes, my dear, that is a dilemma. You see, it's not like a faucet that you can just turn off. But you can let it drip in the background and pay no attention until the sink fills, and then you have to give it your mind."

"Lovely analogy, Mother," her husband says. "In time, Miss Lori, it'll feel as natural as breathing in and out. Now, we'll be leaving tomorrow, but fear not. Young Charlotte will remain here. She has a good ear, that one. You might say perfect pitch for the melody of the spirits. A fine-tuned gift. Never misses a note. Ho! I'm certainly musical today, aren't I, Mother?"

"To be sure, Earl!"

It's all so much to take in, and I have so many questions. I ask only one:

"But — but what happens when someone has crossed over for good?" I start tentatively, feeling a flush of warm hope. "Could I still communicate with him — or her?" Could I feel his lips on mine, his arms around me, after he's vanished forever?

Mr. Crandall removes his straw hat and wipes sweat away with his sleeve. "Well, now, only if the young soldier chooses to be seen and heard; if he thinks it's in your best interest."

My stomach jumps. *They know!*

"But if not," says Mrs. Crandall, her knitting needles ticking, "you can always talk to him in your mind. You just need to take care that you don't get stuck in the past." She's stopped knitting for a second to stare intensely at me.

"This is new ground for me," I murmur.

"Not really, now, is it?" Mr. Crandall says, hanging his hat on his knee. "You've traveled this road before; you're just encountering more traffic now that you're here in Gettysburg where history arises with a flourish."

I don't know what to say. I stare at the ground until I feel Mrs. Crandall pat my arm reassuringly.

"Lori, dear," she says, "I've always been partial to these famous words about love lost. 'Don't cry because it's over; smile because it happened.'"

I look up at her, smiling despite my pain. "Is that Shakespeare?"

"No, dear. Dr. Seuss."

25

DAD'S WATCHING FOR me from the balcony and beats
me to the red front door. My head is still swimming from
everything the Crandalls revealed, and from the discovery of
Wince Carmody's confession — and the ring.

The red flag over the door barely grazes my dad's head as
he offers me a giant towel to wrap around my still-dripping
clothes.

"Lorelei Cordelia, your mother and I would like to have a
word with you."

I follow Dad inside, clutching the towel to me. I feel a pit in my stomach. What do they want to talk to me about? Do they somehow know everything, just like the Crandalls did? Whenever one of my parents talks about having *a word*, it's likely going to be a thousand words, most of which I won't like.

Mom's tapping her foot in the kitchen, with the Chinese takeout cartons all over the table. She's clearing her throat — bad sign — and Dad's fuming. Gertie has the good sense to leave the room. She's never been great at conflict resolution.

Dad begins the inquisition. "It has come to our attention that you've been cavorting with a Battle reenactor, which means he's older than you."

Yeah, about 150 years older. "Cavorting, Dad?"

Mom's turning as pale as a, well, *ghost*. She says, "And there was some mention of . . . murder."

It hits me: Amelia Wilhoit overheard me on the phone with Jos, and quickly reported the conversation to my parents. I struggle to cover for myself by acting indigant. "Mom! Amelia Wilhoit is a romance novelist. She sees vile plots everywhere."

Dad frowns at me. "Yet she distinctly heard the word *murder*, Lorelei, and how you're supposed to solve it. She came to us out of genuine concern for you."

"She's a fake!" I stop just short of calling her a liar. Of course, she wasn't lying.

"Honey, what your father means is, we're wondering who the young man is. We don't mean to pry, but —"

"He's obviously not the boy you went to the dance with, our own Evan Maxwell," Dad puts in.

Gertie trots back into the kitchen at the sound of Evan's name. I think he's been sneaking her bits of hamburger to win her over.

"Who is this boy?" Dad demands.

How do I explain this? Lying to my parents isn't something I do on a regular basis, but this calls for emergency measures. "Okay, you guessed right," I say, thinking quickly as my heart pounds and I clutch the ring in my pocket. "He's a reenactor on the Union side. I met him when I went to watch the Battle on July first." That much is true. Nathaniel and I did meet there that day, even if it wasn't the first time.

"Sit!" Dad says, and Gertie sinks to her haunches, looking guilty. "Not you, Gertie. I meant Lorelei." I slide into a kitchen chair with Dad looming over me, still looking suspicious.

Mom says, "Vernon, why don't you sit down, also. There, that's better."

Dad delivers his usual opening pitch: "You are only sixteen," and I position myself at home plate with my usual catcher comeback: "Almost seventeen."

"Regardless," Dad says. "The point is, we worry about you

going out with boys we haven't met. We've only been here a few weeks. We don't know who these people are, or their families, and so many of the reenactors pour in from all over the country. How can we be sure that you're keeping company with someone reliable who won't take advantage of you, hurt you?"

Nathaniel would never hurt me — I know this now. But anything I say about him, even if I try to make him sound alive and well, will just raise Mom and Dad's suspicions. And it's not like they can call up his parents in Titusville for a friendly meet-and-greet. So my next play is to agree.

"You're right, Mom and Dad. I'll be much more careful starting tomorrow; I promise." Also not a lie.

Dad pats my hand. "I'm afraid that's not good enough, Lorelei."

"What?"

"Your father and I love you and want what's best for you. The problem is, you're such a trusting girl."

How ironic is *that*, since Nathaniel told me just this afternoon that I'm not a trusting soul at all.

"Which is why," Dad adds, "we've decided to ground you for the next forty-eight hours, until all these strangers go back where they came from. Some of them may not be as wholesome as you think."

"You can't do that!" I cry, slapping the table and making the takeout containers quake.

"Yes, Lorelei, we can," Dad says sadly. It's the old *This will hurt me more than it'll hurt you* ploy parents have been using for centuries. "We have to do this for your own protection. You're not to leave the house until July fifth." Dad gets very quiet when he's determined.

I grit my teeth, anger surging through me. "Oh, really? Just see if I'm going to be stripping beds and cleaning toilets in this broken-down, ramshackle rattrap tomorrow when everybody checks out. Not a chance! And that dog upstairs, Brownie? I hope he bites everybody's ankles and they warn all their friends to never come here, and you go broke so Randy doesn't have to see this nuthouse when he comes home from Ghana!" Whew. As soon as the words are all out of my mouth, I feel a stab of guilt and bite my lip, wishing I weren't always so impulsive.

Mom's sigh hasn't got much gusto to it. I'm thinking she doesn't agree with Dad about the grounding, but they always present a united front, so I take a deep breath and play to her weakness out there in left field.

"Mom, tell him," I say, turning to her. "Have I ever done anything to betray your faith in me?"

Mom gives me a thoughtful look. "Well, there was that one time you and Jocelyn snuck into a Phillies game and we got a call from ballpark security — well, no, not really, honey."

"And you haven't had to ground me since I was maybe twelve years old, right, when I dyed my hair puce for Valentine's Day?"

"Irrelevant," Dad jumps in. "This is not punishment, Lorelei. It's for your own safety, the same way we used to put covers over the electric outlets when you were a toddler."

"That's a ridiculous comparison."

"Maybe so." Dad's practically whispering. "But it stands. The morning of July fifth you're free to come and go. Until then, you're grounded. Now, please give me your cell phone."

My jaw drops. "You're putting me under house arrest? Holding me incommunicado? The prisoner doesn't even get her one call?"

"In a sense," he agrees.

I hate you comes to mind, but I've never said that to my parents, even those few times I thought it. But the main, panicky thought now is: If I'm grounded, how will I be able to get to Nathaniel in time?

Dad's hand is out. "Your cell phone, please." I reach under the towel and wheedle the phone out of my pocket. It's ruined anyway, because I forgot it was in there when I sank neck-deep in the creek. I slap the phone into Dad's hand, stand up, and tramp out of the room just as the house phone rings.

Mom answers. "Oh, hello, Evan. Lori can't come to the phone right now. I'm afraid she can't call you later, either. No, she won't be going out tonight. We have family business to take care of. The back area is looking a bit wilted. Will you be watering tomorrow? Great. Have a nice evening, Evan."

She's so *nice* to him, and I'm treated like a felon. How long 'til I'm sprung? An eternity. Well, in the greater scheme of things, not an eternity, I guess. But I'm still furious. I'm thinking *revenge*, inspired by Edison Larch, though I'm not murderous yet. I'm also thinking *freedom, my civil rights*!

I stomp hard on every step to the tower, humiliated. By the time I reach my room, I've hatched a diabolical plan: I'll sneak out the window. They asked for it. It's their fault for treating me like a child when every minute's so crucial. Now that I know who the murderer is, I need to find Nathaniel and help him understand what happened before he vanishes at midnight, forever. I have to, and they can't stop me.

26

I CHANGE INTO a dry scoop-necked T-shirt and jeans, then take out Wince's letter from the ring box and fold it carefully in my pocket. I hide the ring itself next to Dr. Anderson's amputation kit in my pillow.

Next, I walk over to the window. I have an escape hatch: the trellis way below my window. Can I get there? If I can slide down the side of the house from the tower to the third floor without slicing my gut open — which it turns out I can — then I can make it down to the second floor, too. From there it's a stretch, but I can just about reach one foot on the top of the trellis, crushing a bunch of Old Dryden's creeping ivy. Who cares about ivy? I'm just trying not to break a leg, and the whole time I'm frantically concentrating: *Nathaniel, are you reading me?*

Once I'm on solid ground, I run like mad back to the cover of the trees by the creek so Mom and Dad won't see me. I inch farther along the creek and away from the house, waiting for Nathaniel, focusing harder than I ever have to draw him to me. It was so foolish of me to tell him he couldn't hover around or show up in my room. But I'm at the creek to meet him, and he did say he'd be *listening* for me. I'm concentrating so hard, clenching my jaw until my teeth hurt, and my head is starting to throb.

And then I feel that familiar, eerie sense of the air thickening around me, like before a tornado, but the sky is perfectly clear in the early dusk. There's a rustling of leaves and a comforting sense that someone unseen is present. Reaching out, I touch his shoulder where the jagged scar is. He shimmers into the body I know him by. His arms are around me, mine around him, as if nothing could ever come between us. He tilts my chin up. Our lips eagerly find each other, and for that brief moment, I forget that we'll soon be torn apart.

He pulls back a little. "What's wrong, Lorelei?"

No one's ever been that in tune with me. "I'm okay, sort of."
What I have to tell him about Edison and Wince will hurt him.
I try to find the words. They're a bone in my throat.

He's jumpy. I've thrown him off balance. No, it's not that.

"I'm weakening, Lori," he explains, and I feel him shiver. "I
can't hold this form for long."

I wrap my arms around him again, as if I can bind him
together like duct tape on a cracked window. But I know that I
can't, so I release him, but grab his hand. "I have to tell you
something awful, Nathaniel."

His hand is shaking in mine. I grasp his fingers tightly to
stop the shivers. It's as though a sudden fever's come over him.
His face is flushed with heat, his brow is beaded with perspira-
tion, but his hands are ice-cold.

"I know who shot you," I say.

"A stranger. Say it was a stranger, a random bullet." Does
he suspect what I'm about to tell him? I'm silent. He slides his
hand away and looks at me sharply. "It was Edison, wasn't it?"

I make a snap decision not to mention Evan's help in solving the mystery. "Okay, just listen." I decide to read Wince's
letter aloud. I take it from my pocket and unfold it, careful with
the onionskin. As I read, Nathaniel listens with all his energy,
which I know because his body is sagging and his eyelids are
drooping. I'm losing him. My eyes mist, but I have to stay

strong for this. I read him the part about Wince keeping the ring for his own son.

"The ring, President Lincoln's son's ring," Nathaniel murmurs. "So Wince never returned it. He kept it?"

"He did." I've yet to tell Nathaniel I have the ring, up in my room. I read the paragraph about Wince burying the ring after his son died. And then I come to the fourth paragraph of the letter:

"'I refer to my comrade in arms in the 93rd Pennsylvania Infantry, Nathaniel Pierce.'"

He pulls his shoulders tight at the sound of his name. "Yes? Go on."

And I continue reading:

"'I was a party to his fatal wounding at the behest of another soldier whose obsession was vengeance for something over which young Pierce had no control. The culprit, even in the darkest crevice of his soul, professed to be a faithful friend as he pointed his pistol. God save us from such acts of friendship.'"

"It *was* Edison," Nathaniel says, his voice tinged with grief. He rubs a hand over his face like a wand, as if to make the horror go away.

"Nathaniel, listen . . ."

"No, no, you can't shelter me from this any longer. Deep within, I always knew it had to be Edison."

I start to speak again, but Nathaniel puts a finger over my lips to silence me. He's quiet so long that I'm scared his mind has already left me, and only his shell remains. Then he says, "It's because my father made the wisest choices that gave our family every advantage. Edison's father died in the coal-mine explosion, and his family was left penniless. All those years that they suffered paupers' lives, he must have harbored this resentment against me. The ugly pieces fit. Remember, I told you I thought I'd seen him on the battlefield? The doctor said he'd run into someone who knew me. It had to be Edison, yes." Nathaniel's face is contorted in agony.

In a real sense, Nathaniel's right, because it was Edison who intended to kill him. It's just that Edison wasn't the one who fired the gun. What should I say? Should I burden him with the truth that his mortal life ended because of *both* his closest friends? So, I delay. "Horrible as it is, Edison was obsessed with vengeance and waited for the right opportunity to end your life." Somehow, at this point, I just can't use the word *murder.* It feels too cold-blooded, reptilian.

"Why would he want to kill me, though? Why not my father?"

I wonder about that myself and haven't worked out an answer, so we both go silent in thought, until something occurs to me. "Suppose Edison's vengeful grudge wasn't against you at all but against your father. That's why he could shoot you while telling Wince that he was your faithful friend. But he knew that killing you would hurt your father worse than his own death would. Does that make twisted sense?"

"If I had known about the hate in his heart," Nathaniel says, "I'd have found him, made our peace. My father could have helped his family."

"He would have resented that even more."

"I suppose, yes," Nathaniel says solemnly.

"There's one more thing before you —"

"I can't now, Lorelei." His body seems to flicker before me, and my heart stops for a second. "I am much too weak. Let me rest for a little while, and then we will meet again. At the cemetery. At my grave. So we can . . ."

He doesn't have to utter the words *say good-bye*. I know. There's a lump in my throat. I do feel, though, that Evergreen will be the right place to tell him the truth. We'll hold each other, standing there at his grave, with Elizabeth Thorn's statue watching over us, while Nathaniel still has time to process it all before . . .

I blink and notice that Nathaniel is beginning to waver like a desert mirage in the dimming light of dusk.

"No! Don't go yet. Okay, I will meet you at Evergreen."

"Yes. Come to me there just before midnight."

He's fading.

"Forget Rules One, Two, and Three," I yell at the shimmery air. "Come back; come back to me." A fold in the air closes up with the faintest of *snick*s and Nathaniel's gone again. It's almost dark, maybe eight thirty. A few stars dot the sky.

I turn slowly and make my reluctant way back toward the inn. When I'm passing by the shed, a wave of fatigue sweeps over me. I lean against the door of the shed, feeling totally abandoned and trying to get my foggy brain in gear.

There are voices inside the shed. Living people, not the voices of ghosts. Real people are in the shed at this late hour, and they shouldn't be.

There's also noise in the shed that only a carpenter would make — the scritchy sound of nails being pulled out of boards. It's loud enough that anyone inside wouldn't hear my footsteps out here. It's almost dark. I could probably slip by the window unnoticed. It's above my line of vision, although the top of my head might show. I need to see what's going on inside.

The Dutch doors at the back leave a thin swath of space between the top and the bottom. I can't see much this way, since it's about navel-height, but a jerky flashlight in someone's hand reveals a stoop-shouldered man with his head pointed down at the floor. Old Dryden, watching another person wrenching nails out of the floorboards.

This time I know what they're looking for.

27

THE SHED WINDOW'S cracked open for air; otherwise it would be stifling inside. The unseen man growls with the effort and shouts, "This wood's hard as concrete. They think they were building Fort Knox when they put this shack up?"

A woman's voice is too faint for me to make out her words. Maybe she's the one holding the flashlight. Then another woman says, "Used to be a pond. They musta built it strong in case the water ever came back." Bertha.

It's frustrating not to be able to see anything. I have to take a chance and peek in the window. Glad I'm not in the long skirt and corset that Victorian women wore.

How on earth did they sneak around back then?

There's a rain gutter spout to the left of the window. Might hold my weight. I count to ten, steel myself — *now or never* — and climb up. The spout makes a crunching sound and I freeze; did they hear? I have to lean way over to get an instant glimpse inside. Two people plus the Drydens. The second woman is tall and curvy, and I can't see the other man well enough to recognize anything other than a dark blob on the floor, one elbow up in the air with a hammer in his hand. He's swearing like he's in a bar brawl. I step down to the ground, and a section of the spout comes with me.

"Keep the light on the floor, you old geezer!" yells the guy with the hammer.

I climb up on the crushed stump of the gutter and peer in the window again. The light's given me just enough info to see that the second woman is Amelia Wilhoit, the person who got me grounded to keep me away tonight. Is she involved in this hunt for the ring, too? How?

They could all be amateur treasure hunters, making the rounds of stately houses in search of lost booty. I saw that on the Discovery Channel once. But then I remember the article I found online — how the Drydens tried to put one over on that old invalid lady who *misplaced* President Rutherford Hayes's watch. They're not treasure hunters; they're thieves, and specialists, at that. Only presidential plunder.

But why do they expect the ring to be here, in this shed?

Because of something Wilhoit found in her research about the ring being buried underwater? She must have learned all that stuff Evan explained about old ponds morphing into meadowland. The've studied the same map I have, so they figured out that this is where the pond used to be. They connected the dots and got this thug with a hammer to start digging. Even so, they're flying blind, because they don't have the RVA box, which Old Dryden was snooping around in our cellar for. He never found it; I did! And he won't find the ring, either.

But why is Amelia Wilhoit in cahoots with the Drydens? And who is the guy with the hammer? I can't resist one more glimpse, so I climb up on the gutter. Big mistake. The entire thing comes loose from the roof and clatters to the ground.

"Someone's out there," Bertha shouts, before everything goes silent inside. I should run like a gazelle, but instead I do the stupidest thing, I guess because I'm curious to see how it's all going to turn out. Isn't that what Nathaniel said his parents were hovering around for, to see how things turn out?

I flatten myself on the grass, hoping the thieves inside won't spot me in the dark. But it's too late — Old Dryden appears with the flashlight, and terror washes over me. He plants one heavy foot on my back. "Don't think about moving, girlie," he snarls. It feels like my lungs are being crushed, and I can only let out a small whimper. I wish my parents knew I was out here. I wish Nathaniel would come looking for me. Or Evan. Charlotte. *Anyone*. I'm flooded by panic.

I'm also furious, because on my own two feet, I could overtake the Old Dryden gnome. But I'm stupidly and dangerously facedown in the grass with Dryden's foot resting on me like I'm a step stool. My whole body's shaking and I'm choking on my tears of pain and fury. I turn my cheek to capture a little air.

"Tables are turned, girlie, eh?" Dryden says. Then he shouts through the open window. "Hey, come out here and help, Cadmus, come on."

Suddenly, Old Dryden loses his balance, hobbling on one foot, and I have a blessed moment of relief to lift my head and cough. But before I can slither away, the thug from inside the shed, thankfully without his hammer, looms huge above me. He lifts me by the waist so my torso hangs down one side of his massive arm, my legs the other. Hair droops over my face, filling my mouth, which is open, gasping for air. How am I going to get out of this alive? I don't want to join the spirits, not even to be with Nathaniel. *Think. Think!*

Cadmus hauls me into the shed, draped over his arm like I'm a dead cat. Bertha watches warily from the corner.

Cadmus looks around and says, "Amelia, find something to tie her up with good and sturdy."

I hear Wilhoit scurry around on those absurd heels. Blowing my hair out of my eyes, I see with dread that she's found frayed rope and a knife to cut it with. At least I hope that's what the knife is for.

Cadmus drops me onto the ripped-up floor, and pain shoots through my arm. I roll away from a pile of bent nails and splintered boards. The room's spinning; my eyes must be spiraling in my head. Old Dryden holds the flashlight while Cadmus ties my ankles together, then leaves a short lank of rope between my ankles and my wrists, which are also tied together. If I try to loosen my wrists, it'll pull the rope until it cuts into my ankles. And the rope's so short that I wouldn't be able to stand up even if I could wrangle my way to my feet. I want to cry; I want to scream, but I'm paralyzed by fear.

Cadmus lifts me again as if I'm as weightless as a phantom, and then he gruffly tosses me onto the seat of the riding mower. The impact shoots a pain up my spine, which is already bruised from Old Dryden's foot. Another length of rope ties the back of my wrists to the steering wheel. I couldn't possibly control the wheel. What if he turns the mower on, opens the door, and shoves me down the hill toward the creek? Oh God!

I bend my head to rest it on the steering wheel, stretching my back at a punishing angle and tugging on the rope around my ankles. Is this what it's like for a goat to be trussed up before slaughter? Would the goat know what was coming? I can't let my mind go that route. Can't. I close my eyes to think more clearly. Make them believe I'm totally out of it so they can't hurt me any more while I plot my escape.

There's no escape.

But I watch them through slitted eyes anyway. Old Dryden stands guard at my side with the flashlight in his hand. Wilhoit's turning a faded paper every which way. I can only see the back of it; it could be a map, yellowed with age. Now Cadmus is back to pulling up floorboards. Bertha's doing what she does best, which is supervising everyone else, but she seems oddly detached from it all. *Why?* I wonder. *Think. Think!*

"Check again, Amelia," Cadmus is saying. "How many more o' these slats do I need to pull up before I start digging for pay dirt?"

"Just a few more. I'm pretty sure you're in the right spot."

"*Pretty sure* don't cut it, woman."

She holds the map up for Cadmus to see. I only get a flash of it, but it looks hand-drawn, with a big red circle around one spot.

"Hey, Joe, Nature Boy, get your eyes off your gut and tell me, how high's the water table around here? How far down do I have to dig to hit water?"

"Beats me," Old Dryden tells him. "All's I know is that crazy saying: 'With water, everything changes.' Take your time; you're close. Probably."

"That helps a whole lot," Cadmus grumbles. "You're a pack of morons."

And he's the smart one? Then we're all in big trouble.

"Might as well burn the map, Amelia. It ain't doing us a whit of good."

"I don't think so, sweetheart."

Sweetheart? So, this Cadmus guy is her boyfriend? Suddenly, I remember the framed photograph on Wilhoit's desk — yes, that was Cadmus! For a romance writer, she's got rotten taste in men.

"I said burn the paper, woman. Here, reach in my pocket. There's a lighter."

Wilhoit obeys — I would have fought him, I think. She flicks the lighter with shaking hands that hold the brittle map by a corner, until there's nothing but ash and a hot speck of paper, which she tosses away from herself rather than singe her fingertips. Eying the flammable fertilizer bags along one wall, I send up a quick prayer: *Don't let the embers ignite the whole shed.*

I'm miserably uncomfortable; every muscle is pulling. I can't help it; I let out a groan. Cadmus looks up sharply, wielding the hammer like a caveman club. "Give 'er the chloroform," he orders Wilhoit.

My stomach clenches in terror. *No!*

Wilhoit grabs a rag and pours a clear liquid onto it. The familiar sweet, pungent smell lingers on the air as she struts over to me. Did the frogs on our dissecting table at school suspect what was in store for them like I do? Frogs, goats — why are animals cluttering my mind when I need to be alert for human error?

One of her heels catches on a splintered board, and she falls headlong to the floor, bellowing in pain. A loose nail's pierced her arm. If I weren't so uncomfortable, not to mention terrified, I'd cheer and laugh.

Cadmus curses again and shouts, "Clumsy broad, you're gonna asphyxiate us."

"I'm bleeding to death over here! I need a tetanus shot." Wilhoit tries to scramble to her feet with Bertha's help, still clutching the chloroform bottle. At least she didn't fling the deadly poison all over the room and knock us all out.

Bertha wrenches the bottle out of Wilhoit's hand, muttering, "Too chancy. Nobody knows when a little bit's too much."

I swallow hard. Did Bertha just save my life?

"It's the plan, Bertha, remember?" Old Dryden barks. "What we decided if anybody butted in on our work. There's a fortune at stake. Think I want to sweat in rich people's gardens forever?" Old Dryden extends his hand. "Give it here."

Bertha grasps the bottle with both hands behind her back, walking backward toward the window. "Twelve years I've wasted with you and your snoring. Bah! All of you, you're a posse of psychos."

She's sane? I'm praying she'll toss the bottle out the window. *Please. Please.* But Cadmus comes up behind her.

"Hand it over, Ma."

Ma? Cadmus is her son? I should have guessed. Crazy breeds crazy, even if Bertha is acting somewhat rational now. And that explains why I thought Cadmus looked familiar in that photo on the desk — he bears a striking resemblance to Bertha.

She jerks her shoulder away from him, so he snatches the bottle and rag out of her hands. Bertha fires me a look that says, *I'm sorry, kid. I gave it my best shot.*

The bottle's open. I watch Cadmus hold his breath so he won't inhale any of the chloroform as he opens the bottle and pours some onto the rag and slams it onto my face. I try to spit it away; my tongue can't avoid its hot, sweet taste. My head's reeling. How long can I resist? I can't hold my breath forever. . . .

28

MY HEAD ROLLS like a pumpkin on the vine, or maybe more like a cannonball shot during the Battle. My eyes are starting to close just as the door bangs open and the shed's flooded with light. As if from a great distance, I hear voices shouting, "Police! Nobody move a muscle!"

Cadmus, thankfully, doesn't listen. He jumps away from me, but the rag clings to my face. I try to shake it off, which is taking monumental effort as my body yields to the chloroform.

"Drop to the ground, all of you." I hear thuds all around the shed as I draaaaag my head slowly toward the door. There are the Crandalls, right behind two cops.

Mrs. Crandall says, "See, Earl, I told you our girl was in peril."

"How right you were, Mother," her husband replies, while the second cop is making his way around the prone forms of Bertha, Old Dryden, Wilhoit, and Cadmus. And then I see Evan right behind Mrs. Crandall. He sizes up the situation immediately, and he pulls the cloth off my nose and mouth. I can breathe again, but my head still seems to be dangling from my neck like an anchor. Evan starts to untie me. The other cop stops him, saying, "We gotta take some shots." Camera shots, I'm relieved to know. "Don't move, any one of you down there eating sawdust."

The cop keeps one foot on Cadmus, obviously the biggest and baddest guy in the shed, and pulls out a small camera. He clicks madly all around the room, while the other cop keeps his gun aimed steadily.

In my muddled state, I see Old Dryden wildly swinging the flashlight. The cop with the gun lurches for him and wrestles his wrists into handcuffs behind him.

Bertha's wimpering, "Go easy, he's got scoliosis and a heart murmur."

Evan spots the knife on the floor and reaches for it to cut me loose, but a cop snatches it up with his handkerchief, muttering, "Fingerprints." Evan's cleared to free me with the covered knife, and he slices through the ropes carefully. My whole body goes limp with relief and the morning-after fog of the chloroform, and I collapse into Evan's arms. The rag's now in an evidence bag. Both cops are handcuffing the rest of the culprits. I'm watching through droopy-lidded eyes, my limp and achy body supported by Evan in the doorway, where I'm sucking in sweet, fresh air.

The words come so slowly: "How . . . did you . . . know?" I ask him.

"Easy," he says quietly. This isn't meant for the cops. "I called your cell, but you didn't answer. So, I tried the house phone. Your mom sounded kind of distracted. When she said you wouldn't be going out tonight, couldn't even talk on the phone, I knew something was up. This is your last night to solve the murder case, right? I knew you'd do anything to get the job done. For Nathaniel," he adds.

The Crandalls come up behind us, and Mrs. Crandall says, "I was frantic. I just knew Lori was in trouble, and we'd need all the help we could get, short of Lori's parents, who would be beside themselves with worry."

"You did the right thing, Mother," Mr. Crandall says, beaming at his wife.

"So, when Mrs. Crandall called me, she insisted that I come over right away, said she'd already called 9-1-1." Evan takes a cloth out of his pocket and starts to wipe my brow, but I panic, reliving the drugged rag on my face.

"Relax, Lori, it's just a nice, clean handkerchief. You're sweating like a pig."

"Pigs . . . don' swea'," I manage. "No swea' glans."

"That's my friend Lori. Always gotta be right." He smiles, his teeth blindingly white, and he hugs me tighter. "Let me check with the cops. I want to take you back to your parents."

"Uh-uh. They'll . . . go . . . bonkers. Grounded . . . snuck out."

The cops are marching the handcuffed four across the lawn to the two backup cars at the end of the driveway. Somewhere in my smoggy mind I think, *Wow, just like on* Law & Order.

One cop asks me, "You okay, miss? We can call for an ambulance."

I shake my head, which is starting to feel better now that I've breathed in the fresh air. "I'm okay. Jus' godda . . . go . . . home."

"Your parents up at the house?"

"Yezzir."

"All right, then. Let's go. What are your names, you and your folks?"

I can't remember theirs. I'm not sure I can pull my own name out in my fuzzy, muddled state.

Evan answers, "Her name's Lori Chase. Her parents are Vernon and Miriam Chase." He supports me, staggering toward the house just as the door flies open and everyone pours out — the McLeans, the Durnings — all staring at the cops and me. Mr. McLean has his arms around Jake and Max like a harness. The boys are in pj's, rubbing sleep out of their eyes, and Brownie's nipping at everyone's heels.

Mom cuts through the crowd and throws her arms around me. "Oh my God, what happened? Lori? I thought you were upstairs in your room. Vernon!" she shouts toward the hall. "Come quick, Lori's hurt!"

Dad flies out the door, waving a newspaper. "What happened, Lorelei? What happened to her?" Dad asks frantically as Evan releases me into Dad's arms. Dad walks me inside, one cop follows, and Mom closes the door on all our guests.

I'm thinking, *Not good for repeat business,* as I'm lowered to a sofa in the parlor. Nothing I want more than sleep right now. *Have to stay awake. Why? Something to do. What? Something to tell the cop. What is it? What?* Bertha.

"Of'cer, older woman, not like uh res' of 'em. She . . . she tried tuh help me."

The cop nods. "We'll take that into consideration. You gotta be sure to keep the girl awake 'til her head clears," he advises Mom and Dad.

Someone's knocking on the red door. Dad lets the McLeans and the Durnings and Crandalls in, motioning them right upstairs without a word. I'm betting the boys are listening from the landing.

But then Evan steps inside and Dad doesn't send him home right away.

"Mr. and Mrs. Chase, can we go into another room to talk?" the cop is asking.

Mom's frightened eyes are fixed on me. "I don't want to leave her alone."

But Dad says what I'm already thinking. "Evan can watch her," he offers, and I manage to nod my assent.

"Soon as possible, we'll get Lori here to the ER for a checkup," the cop is telling Evan. "Right now, get her a Coke or some coffee."

"I'll do it!" Mom cries before Evan can make a move. Frantically, she runs to the kitchen, and returns in a flash with a glass of sugary Pepsi. Then she and Dad follow the cop into the adjoining room while Evan sits down beside me.

He holds the drink to my lips. Yuck, it's warm; no ice. I think of Wince, trying to help heal Nathaniel in the tent, moments before he accidentally shot him dead.

"It'll give you a good caffeine charge to counteract the chloroform," Evan urges me gently. "Drink gustily. So, do you want to tell me how it all went down in the shed?"

I take a few sips of the warm soda, and I do feel my head start to clear. But time's all skewed like when I had my appendix out two years ago, and I was resurfacing after the anesthetic. It feels like all the shed stuff happened yesterday, or a month ago, or a minute ago, or hasn't happened yet, but will. After a few more gulps of the soda, I sputter out the details about the Drydens and Cadmus and Wilhoit tearing up the shed to find the buried ring. It's so hard to get the words out, and I can't imagine what they sound like on the other end of the tunnel, but I say something that resembles, "You're a real cowboy, Evan Maxwell. You got there just in time to rescue the damsel in distress."

"Just cowboy? I think I rank superhero status. Batman, Superman, the Hulk. At least Robin. Actually, you have Superwoman Crandall to thank for getting me on the scene."

The fog's starting to lift. Time's returning to the current dimension. I jolt up to a sitting position, causing my head to swarm with bees inside. Out the window I see the roof lights of police cars spinning red lights round and round, like my head. I close my eyes to slow the swirling. My parents and the cop are talking low in the other room, like more buzzing bees, and then Dad rushes back and says, "The officers will take you and your mom to the hospital. I'll follow in the Taurus."

I shake my head vigorously. Those bees go nuts until I think my head's going to explode, but at least the red-light cars are leaving now.

Mom runs down the stairs with a small bag of supplies. "Toothbrush, nightie, and comb, in case they admit you, honey."

I start to protest but Dad pats my arm. "No argument, Lorelei," he says gently. "Just leave it in our hands." He turns to Evan. "Thank you, son, for looking after her. We'll call you when we know what's going on."

"If you don't mind, Mr. and Mrs. Chase, I'll wait right here."

"It's nine o'clock, son. We might not be back for a couple hours," Dad says, fishing his car keys out of his pocket.

A couple hours? My eyes fly open, race wildly. *I have to get to Evergreen Cemetery before midnight!*

"All the same, sir, I'll wait here 'til Lori comes home," Evan says, giving me a reassuring look. And somehow, it helps. A little.

29

THE ER'S A madhouse. What's going on here?" Dad asks the policewoman who's cutting through a mob to get me to the check-in desk. The waiting room is small and crawling with people moaning and coughing.

"Last Battle night," Officer Foley says — she introduced herself to me as we were leaving the inn. "The kooks are out. Wait 'til next week when all the bikers are in town. Hogs all over the parking lot."

In a few minutes, she scores us a quick sit-down with the triage nurse, who immediately shuffles me into the back room while people in the waiting room watch me, probably wondering what horrific thing I did to get busted.

And then Mom and Dad and I are in a tiny examining room. They've pulled a three-quarter-length curtain around us, and I watch Officer Foley's clompy shoes pacing back and forth on the other side of the curtain. We wait and wait. I hear the pizza-sized clock at the nurses' station click; valuable minutes tick by.

Finally, a nurse comes in, asks a thousand questions, does the usual stuff (blood pressure, temperature), tells my parents to step out to the waiting room while she asks me a protocol of questions about whether I've been abused in any way, or if there's anything personal I want to tell her that I can't say in front of my parents.

There's a lot, but it has nothing to do with how my body's working, so I say, "No, let's get on with the exam."

A nurse-practitioner does a preliminary neuro-exam that consists of me following his finger as it wags back and forth, counting backward from a hundred by sevens and giving him the day, date, and time. Man, do I know that one. Tuesday, July third; dangerously close to midnight. I assure him that the fog's lifted, and I'm ready to go home. Not yet. They take X-rays of my back and prick my arm so they can take blood. I barely feel the pain and discomfort. After what I went through earlier tonight, it's nothing. And it's clean, quiet, and orderly in here. Not like it was for those soldiers who laid their arms bare for a fast, brutal amputation. *Piles of limbs out the window.* I think of Nathaniel, ache for him.

A Dr. Biao comes in, looks over the chart, listens to my lungs and heart, and proclaims them to be in good shape. She doesn't know that my heart is about to be broken in ways her cold stethoscope couldn't possibly pick up.

Mom and Dad fill out papers, the cop fills out more papers, and I'm sprung from the hospital. It's past ten thirty. So little time left.

At home, Evan's waiting in the parlor. He jumps to his feet and gives me a hug.

"I have to go to Evergreen," I whisper to him.

"I know," he whispers into my hair. "That's why I'm here."

"Thanks for waiting for us, Evan. Now I need to take Lori upstairs and settle her into bed," Mom says, obviously dismissing Evan.

"No!" I turn to my parents, pleading at them with my eyes. "There's something I have to do first. I can't explain this now, but I have to get to Evergreen Cemetery. I have to — to say good-bye to someone."

"You're not going anywhere, Lorelei Cordelia." Dad doesn't sound angry, though, just worried.

I'm pulling myself together, trying to appear as rational as possible. That's not easy when my whole reason for going to Evergreen is to meet with a person who was buried there a century and a half ago and who's about to return to the spirit world.

"Dad, after this I'll stay grounded, I promise."

Grounded, groundhog, planted deep in the cemetery ground — all related to what I have to do.

"I'll give up my cell phone for a month," I continue. "Stay off Facebook for the rest of my natural life. Well, maybe not that long. But this is something I absolutely have to do, trust me, and it has to be done right now, before midnight."

"Grounded isn't the issue, Lorelei." Dad sounds confused, which is unusual for him. He glances toward Evan. "Do you know what this is about?"

"Yes, sir, I do."

"Mind telling me?"

"Not at this time, sir."

"I see. And in your estimation, it's essential that Lorelei get to this cemetery place?"

"Yes, sir, I believe it is."

"You just have to trust me on this, Dad. I'll explain everything tomorrow."

Mom speaks up, wringing her hands. "I'm very uneasy about this, honey."

"I'll go with her," Dad offers, to console Mom.

"No! You just wouldn't understand. Please, Dad."

Mom and Dad exchange looks again while he's processing. He's a good and quick processor. "Will you go with her, Evan? See that she's safe?"

I turn my pleading eyes toward Evan, but then I realize he's already two steps ahead of me. He takes a deep breath and responds, "I'll watch out for her, Mr. and Mrs. Chase."

"All right, then," Dad concedes, checking his watch. "Your mother and I want you back here by twelve thirty, and if you're not, I'll come get you myself. Clear, Lorelei Cordelia?"

"Clear, Dad. Thank you a million times over."

"I hope I don't regret this," he mutters.

I hug Dad and Mom before they can change their minds, and Evan and I hurry outside.

We settle into the yellow Camaro wreck. On the way to the cemetery, Evan doesn't say a word. I can guess what this is costing him, this middle-of-the-night trek for Nathaniel, but I can't focus on Evan's feelings right now. I'm concentrating fiercely on conjuring Nathaniel's spirit to meet me at Evergreen, as he promised. The rattletrap Camaro grinds to a halt just outside the Evergreen gatehouse. In the dark of night, flood-lights illuminate the red brick. But in Elizabeth Thorn's time, no electric light would have streamed through the windows to unsettle those children sleeping inside. I picture her barefooted, wispy hair loose to her waist, pacing up and down a narrow hall. She's worrying about whether her husband will return from the war hundreds of miles away.

I have to get her out of my mind so I can be fully focused in the *now*, ready for what lies ahead — the truth about Wince and the farewell. Both I dread.

I look into the darkness of the cemetery. "Am I too late?"

"It's eleven forty-five. But hey, maybe ghosts don't operate on daylight saving time." Evan pulls a flashlight from the glove box. "I know the cemetery. My grandfather's buried here. What section do you have to go to?"

"His grave is in the oldest part. He'd have been buried only a few years after the cemetery opened." I know my way around the cemetery, too, or at least I thought I did — everything looks so different in the dark, so . . . forbidding. "Near the Jenny Wade statue with the perpetual flag." Jenny Wade was the only civilian killed during the Battle, when a random bullet found her inside her sister's house. She was only a few years older than me.

"This way." Evan holds my hand to guide me into the cemetery. We pass right by the statue of Elizabeth Thorn, which is barely visible in the black night, yet I feel her as if she were try-ing to wrestle her way out of the bronze.

Evan and I weave around tombstones and ground that's knotted with roots. All I can do is follow his beam, hoping a jolt of recognition will alert me when I'm in the right place. Where Nathaniel is buried. Where Nathaniel will be waiting.

"Evan, stop. I need to do this alone."

"I know. I'll get you there, wherever *there* is, and then I'll go sit with my grandpa. Haven't visited him in a long time. When you're ready to leave, raise the flashlight toward the sky and wave it in a big, slow circle. I'll come get you."

We slide in and out between headstones with strangers' names engraved on them, some so old that the engraving is barely readable and the granite corners are worn and round as stooped shoulders.

"Anything?" Evan asks.

"Not yet." And then there is something: a sudden drop in temperature and that feeling that the air is thrumming with presence. I stop suddenly, listening. No words, but I know Nathaniel's here. "This is the place, Evan."

"Sure?"

"Please, there isn't much time."

He hands me the flashlight and backs away, watching to make sure I'm safe.

He's a shadowy moving figure among the still, cold grave-stones, until he disappears into the darkness. I click off the flashlight to preserve the battery. At least, that's what I tell myself, but it's really because I won't need light to see Nathaniel.

He's light itself.

30

I'M HERE, LORELEI." Nathaniel reaches for my hand, still warm from Evan's. He gently tugs me to the ground until we're sitting side by side, our backs against his gravestone. He and I have spent so much time leaning against granite boulders and tombstones. Odd way to be *dating*, if you can call it that. "I'm sorry I didn't come sooner," I tell him, holding tight to his hand. He does seem more substantial than he did when we spoke earlier — the rest must have done him good.

Nathaniel nods, his eyes full of concern. "I know what happened tonight in that small building up the hill. You asked me to *listen for you*, and so I have been with you for the past three hours. I heard you plead with your parents to let you come here. I guided you to this very spot."

Did he? Or did Evan? I was so scared, Nathaniel."

"I know, my Lorelei." He's restless beside me, a final burst of nervous energy. Maybe he's *all* energy. How will he take what I have to tell him? I choke on my own words: "I nearly died. Would you want me to be dead so we could stay together?"

He's quiet. Do I need to repeat the question, or is it just too hard for him to answer? Then he speaks. "I've been around a long, long time, Lorelei, bumbling around in your world of talking machines, some big ones and some small enough to nearly swallow, and lights so bright they sear my eyes. I don't belong in the twenty-first century, not even the twentieth. But some things are timeless, and one of them is this: Love is not selfish. You're sixteen."

"Nearly seventeen," I protest out of habit.

"You have a whole life ahead of you. It severely unnerved me when I thought you were going to leave your body too soon. Yes, I would've welcomed you with open heart. I couldn't, though. You had to return to your life. I knew it wasn't your time to cross over. So I sent a thought to a lady named Mrs. Crandall, who heard my plea." He turns my face toward him. "I had to save you. I had to let you go."

Right now I'd leave everything behind and go with him. We are sitting so close together and I grip his hand. He must sense what I'm feeling because he unlaces his fingers from mine. "We are here to say good-bye," he reminds me softly. "Well, here in this moment. Not here in the sense of here in this universe. In the endless loop of time and space."

I have to smile at that, even though my heart is shattering. "That's the basic difference between us, isn't it, Nathaniel? You're cruising through eternity, and I'm firmly grounded in the earth beneath my feet."

He reaches for my hand again. "You are very grounded, Lorelei. But you are also connected to me, and to the spirit world. That is why you are one of a kind."

I blush in the darkness, then shake my head, coming back to reality. "We're not here just to say good-bye, Nathaniel," I tell him, fighting back tears. "I have to finish telling you everything."

"First tell me how everything fits together about what happened in that small building, when the world almost lost you."

I sprint through the horrors in the shed: the Drydens, their son Cadmus, and his girlfriend, Amelia Wilhoit. How they were desperate to find the ring to cash it in for a small fortune. "They don't know that I have it. No one else knows but you and me."

"And Evan Maxwell."

"Yes, Evan."

I can sense Nathaniel weakening by the second, no more solid than a helium balloon. If I squeeze his arm, my fingers will meet in the center of his flesh. Let go of him, and he'll float up to the sky. There will be no string to pull him back to me.

Only minutes left. The closer we get to midnight, the less of him I'll have to hold on to. "There's one last thing I have to tell you, Nathaniel." My blood is roaring in my ears and I have to force myself to get the words out. "It's about Wince." I take both his hands in mine; they're no heavier than a rag doll's.

"This is really hard to do."

"What? What is it?" His eyes lock on mine until I have to lower my head.

A deep breath fills me with a few seconds of courage. "That night, before you were shot, you were unconscious or delirious. Even if you hadn't been, you couldn't have seen what was going on behind your back, because Wince sat you up to spoon some more healing tea into your mouth. Edison burst into the tent, his gun loaded, determined to make your family pay for his family's suffering."

"Yes, we've been through all this before," Nathaniel says urgently.

The courage has abandoned me, so I swallow deeply and rush through the rest. "Wince struggled with Edison —" I stop, seeing Nathaniel's face contorted with grief. I don't want to reveal this awful fact to him. And yet, he's waited a hundred and fifty years for the truth. "The two of them tumbled to the ground. Wince ripped the gun out of Edison's hand and . . . and . . ."

Nathaniel pulls my hands to his lips. His words vibrate through my trembling fingers. "Wince pulled the trigger, is that what you're telling me?"

Softly, I say, "Yes. I'm so sorry. It was a terrible accident."

Nathaniel settles into himself, silent and separate from me for a few seconds. His voice is wavery, but he manages to say the most astonishing thing. "Don't you see, Lorelei? I would have been dead either way. But Wince allowed me to travel into the next world with dignity, at the hand of a true friend, not a bitter enemy. And all these years I didn't know."

It takes me a moment, but now I can see it the same way he does. There's no need to burden him with the knowledge that Wince suffered in guilt all the rest of his days. Nathaniel, at least, is at peace. I take my hands back and fold them calmly in my lap as he speaks quickly, the energy leeching away from him.

"Do you know whose family plot this is?" He pulls me to my feet and turns me toward the four headstones in a straight row, like a pew. Nathaniel's gravestone is here at our end, then there's a bit of space before the next two, which are nearly touching, like lovers' shoulders. The farthest one is small. A child's? I shine the flashlight, careful not to lift the light all the way up so Evan sees my signal. Not yet.

The letters carved in the granite are faint, but I can make them out. Next to Nathaniel's grave is Vienna Joost Carmody, 1844–1901. Beside her lies Winston Jeremiah Carmody, 1841–1904. And at the end, the smaller marker:

NATHANIEL JONATHAN CARMODY
1865–1865
BELOVED SON
THERE IS A GILDED ROOM IN THE MANSION OF HEAVEN
FOR THOSE TAKEN TOO EARLY

Tears fill my eyes. "Oh, Nathaniel! He named his son for you."

Nathaniel's quiet, staring at the small gravestone.

"Vince was a true friend," Nathaniel says. "No matter what really happened that night. He was not like Edison Larch, deranged with vengeance."

There is so much more to say, and also little more that we can say to each other. He speaks quickly: "You've given me the serenity I've sought for a century and a half, Lorelei. I'll be eternally grateful. I'll not need to return to this place year after year." He puts his arm around my waist; his arm is nearly weightless. I feel him shimmering, like moonlight on water. "I love you, Lorelei. I think I've loved you for a thousand centuries."

"I love you, too, Nathaniel." My voice is thick with tears and trembling. "Will we ever meet again?"

"Again and again," he assures me, "but not here, and not as Nathaniel and Lorelei. Now, it grieves me deeply, but I must leave you. There's one last thing I'm asking you to do for me."

"Anything."

"Evan Maxwell. He's a good man, and he cares for you. Give him a corner of your heart — will you do that for me, my Lorelei?"

I nod. Nathaniel pulls me toward him. I turn into his embrace. That jagged scar on his right shoulder shimmers under my fingers, assuring me that he was once truly flesh and blood. I lift my eyes to look into his. They're nearly lifeless black pools now. I'm losing him second by second. His lips brush mine like a feather. He gently lifts my arms off his shoulders, kisses my palms, and lowers my arms to my sides.

He backs away. Two steps and he's already blended into the night, into timeless eternity. I wait alone, hugging my own shivering body a few aching minutes before I raise the flashlight heavenward.

31

EVAN ASKS NO questions in the car back to Coolspring. Mom and Dad also give me a pass when they see my zombie expression. Mom walks me upstairs, helps me into my pj's, and lets Gertie sleep at the foot of my bed. Gertie keeps glancing at Mom to ask, *Really? You mean it?*

I slide my pillow down to the other end of the bed and curl around Gertie, so glad not to be alone tonight.

• • •

In the morning, wildfire gossip rampages through the house. Everyone's buzzing about the cops at our door and the events in the shed. I learn from Dad that Amelia Wilhoit, Cadmus, and Old Dryden are behind bars. Bertha's been released but warned not to leave the county. She may stand trial along with the others.

I'm not talking, just serving breakfast robotically, still deep in the grief and confusion of last night. People are trying not to stare at me and the sunglasses that hide my bloodshot, swollen eyes.

Dad whispers over a stack of dirty dishes, "We're going to have to talk about it, you know."

Everyone's checking out — going to spend the Fourth at the Poconos or somewhere more festive, no doubt — so the inn is starting to feel weird and empty. It's Independence Day, but I feel trapped.

After the McLeans leave — vowing to come back next summer — my parents and I settle in the parlor. I know what's coming, but I'm too numb with sadness to worry about their interrogation.

"Miriam, please put the feather duster aside and sit and relax," Dad says. "You too, Lorelei. Where would you like to start?"

Yeah, where? Feed it to them slowly so they don't mentally choke on it? I mean, they're great parents, but they're living in another century. They're probably a lot like Nathaniel's parents. I take a deep breath and plunge into the shallow end: "So, now you realize that Amelia Wilhoit really can't be trusted."

"At least she alerted us to something we should know about," Mom says.

"Who is this boy you've been meeting, and how old is he?" Dad demands.

What can I tell them that won't make them crazy? The truth, but something just short of the *whole* truth. "His name is Nathaniel Pierce. Nineteen." At least he was, in 1863.

"From Gettysburg?" Dad asks. "Have we met his family?"

"No, he's from Punxsutawney, Pennsylvania, like the groundhog. Can we talk about this later? There's a lot more we have to deal with now. The shed, for starters."

"Yes," Mom affirms. "The police sketched it out for us, but we're in the dark about your role in the whole thing. Enlighten us, please."

So, I ramble on about Old Dryden in the cellar and Dr. Anderson's amputation kit and Vince and the Lincoln ring. I explain how Evan was my partner in investigating everything, and this seems to please them. But they are also concerned.

"Oh, Lorelei, you expect us to buy into this fantastical idea that the ring belonged to President Lincoln?" Dad asks, frowning.

"It did; it came off the finger of Lincoln's son, William. He was eleven when he died. I know it for a fact." If Wikipedia is factual.

"Honey, if this ring is the genuine article, it would be quite valuable, wouldn't it?" Mom asks.

"Yes! That's what the Drydens and Amelia Wilhoit were looking for last night, why they tore up the garden shed," I explain. "There used to be a pond there. They thought the ring had been buried underwater."

Dad gives me his narrowed eyes, the kind that say, *What are you hiding?* "Where is this ring now, Lorelei?"

I hesitate. "If I tell you where it is, you'll take it away like you did my cell phone." That's a low blow, which Dad sidesteps.

He sighs. "Today's the Fourth of July. Nothing will be open, but tomorrow I'll call the Lincoln Library to inquire about this find. You'll have that ring in the palm of my hand by tomorrow, right?"

Saved by the Crandalls! Mr. Crandall comes down the stairs, a suitcase in each hand. Mrs. Crandall trails behind with her Macy's bag stuffed with orange knitting.

"Splendid timing," Dad mutters.

Mr. Crandall says, "It's been an inspiration spending these days with you, Chases. Put us in your book for General Buford next July. We'll make it an annual tradition, shall we, Mother?"

"To be sure!" Mrs. Crandall winks at me and says, "Look to the future, my dear."

"Good advice, Mother, but let's remember, the future isn't what it used to be. Tallyho, Chases! Happy Fourth!"

As soon as they're gone, my parents turn to me again. This time, it's Mom who starts the interrogation, but it's not about the ring.

"I'm still confused about something, Lori. This boy, Nathaniel. What is the story on him?"

I take a deep breath.

"Okay, remember when I was ten and I told you Great-Grandpa Tunis sang 'Take Me Out to the Ball Game' after he was dead?"

Mom nods. "We thought it was adorable that you imagined such a thing, Lori."

"He sang it to me. I heard him. I saw him. I wasn't sure back then. I know it now."

Mom and Dad exchange a parental glance that looks like it means, *Get a shrink on speed dial.*

"Gettysburg brings this spirit thing out in people," I explain. "I mean, six thousand soldiers died here in three days, and another twenty-five thousand were wounded. It gets to you if you let it. I've had other experiences like Great-Grandpa Tunis," I admit, but I don't tell them about the boy in the crystal ball. Not yet.

Dad says quietly, "Your mother and I do not talk to dead people, nor do they talk to us. Why you?"

"It's not like it's inherited, like dimples or big feet. I'm just lucky, I guess. Or not."

Mom asks, "Has Randy heard about this?"

"He says I'm on the *kalunga* line. That's a West African thing, the line between the living and the dead. It's not either/ or. It's two parts of the same thing."

"The *kalunga* line," Dad mutters. "Where do our kids get these ideas, Miriam?"

I can't back down now. "It's a gift of second sight. Charlotte has it, too, by the way. And so do the Crandalls. For me, it's been in there all my life. It just never got totally switched on before we came here. Like when you get a new cell phone, and you can't use it until it's activated. Coming here to Gettysburg activated my circuits. I've had some pretty strange experiences this week, and Nathaniel is the most amazing."

"Nathaniel, the boy you like from Punxsutawney?" Mom says.

"Yes. He was a Union soldier, here during the Battle."

"What?" They both gasp it together.

I nod, standing tall. "I fell in love with him during the Battle Days."

"With a ghost? In three days?" Dad shouts. He sinks into his chair and blows air out his mouth. "This is more than I can handle without pastry, Miriam — lots of it, the gooier the better. In fact, give it to me intravenously."

Mom heads for the emergency stash of cream puffs in the freezer.

"Don't think of Nathaniel as a ghost," I say. "Think of him as a spirit."

"There's a difference?" Dad asks in disbelief.

"Yes. And, look — for spirits, a day that they're here on earth is a bigger slice of eternity. I've been operating on their timetable the last week, not ours."

As Mom comes into the room with the mini cream puffs, Dad says, "This Nathaniel person, he's who you met at the cemetery?"

"Yes, to say good-bye." So, I unload most of the rest — how Nathaniel was murdered and how he asked me to solve the murder; about Edison Larch and Wince Carmody and the four graves; and how it's all related to Lincoln's ring.

Dad's popping one mini cream puff after another into his mouth, and Mom's breathing like an asthmatic, but on the whole, they're handling this pretty well, for parents.

The dark shadows are lengthening up in my tower room. My parents have gone into town to see the fireworks, and didn't push when I said I'd rather stay home and rest. I've already e-mailed both Jocelyn and my brother all the updates about what happened, not quite having the energy to talk to them each about it. Once Jos is back from camp, and Randy back from Africa, I'll be able to sit down with them both, face-to-face, and discuss everything. By then, hopefully, time will have healed my wounds a little, too.

I gaze out the window, wishing I could watch the fireworks with Nathaniel, and wondering if he can see them from wherever he is. Then I think of Evan. Of the promise I made to Nathaniel. Ever since the incidents of last night, Evan has *gotten* it — that he should make himself scarce while Mom and Dad and I figure out what's next. But I know he's waiting to hear from me. I decide to give him a call, and he picks up right away.

"Hello?"

"Hi. It's Gloomy Glinda."

I hear the smile in his voice. "Tough times, huh?"

"Can you meet me at the creek?"

"Be there in ten."

On the bank, I drag my feet through troubled water that reflects the darkening sky and my darker mood. Evan comes and sits beside me, doesn't say a word, waits.

"Thanks for everything," I tell him finally. "What would I have done without you, Evan? You're a really nice guy."

He grins. "*Reliable*. Like my old Camaro."

I nudge him in the side just as the fireworks start booming overhead. We watch the dazzling display of reds, whites, blues, and golds. We're silent, our faces tilted upward, but I don't resist when Evan reaches for my hand, guides my head to his shoulder, and locks his arm around me. I'm surprised to real- ize that we fit together. Our feet swish through the cool water in sync.

"Would you like to have dinner tomorrow night?" Evan asks. "I'll take you to Dobbin House."

"I'm not sure," I tell him truthfully. Everything still feels like such chaos inside. With the wrenching memory of say- ing good-bye to Nathaniel, I'm not sure I'm really ready to move on.

"Okay, let me know tomorrow," Evan says, his tone reassuring. I understand that he's fine with waiting, and for that I am grateful. We sit together at the creek until the night air turns cool and it's time for us to part ways.

First thing the next morning, while Charlotte is polishing the parlor furniture, Dad calls the Lincoln Library and connects with someone who seems to know what he's doing. Charlotte, Mom, and I watch a dozen expressions flicker across Dad's face until he says, "I see. Well, thank you," and he lays the Victorian phone in its cradle in slow motion.

"Well, Vernon?" Mom asks.

Dad's clearly shocked. "The library already owns the ring that belonged to William Lincoln."

"What?" I whisper, my stomach dropping.

"And what about the ring Lori found?" Mom asks.

Dad shakes his head. "He's heard about this other ring, which surfaces every few years like an urban legend, but it's bogus. So much for financing Lorelei's college education by selling it to the Lincoln Library for a million bucks. It's worthless."

I'm deep in thought. Charlotte leaves the room, saying she has an errand to run, and I go upstairs to have another look at the ring, wondering if it'll seem any different to me now. When I shake my spare pillow, the RVA amputation kit tumbles out, and Wince's onionskin letter, but there's no ring bag under it. I rip the sheets off my bed, dump the two pillows out of the cases, and slap around under the bed feeling for the ring. All I find is my bat, which I roll across the floor.

I'm crushed, even if that ring never dug into the flesh of William Lincoln's feverish finger — even if it *is* worthless — because the ring is my memory of Nathaniel. But it's gone, just like Nathaniel.

Later, I'm trudging downstairs when I bump into Charlotte on the third-floor landing. "I have something for you," she says, arm deep into her bag. She pulls out a small package wrapped in a soft red maple leaf and tied with gold thread. It looks out of place, like an enchanted relic from a distant time. We sit down on the chaise below a shelf full of Gettysburg history books. Her face glowing, Charlotte motions for me to open the package.

My hand's shaky as I untie the thread. The leaf falls open to reveal a small green silk bag, which sends my heart racing. I recognize this bag!

"How did you . . . ?" I ask, glancing at Charlotte.

"I borrowed it as a favor to · · · a friend of yours."

"Nathaniel?"

She only smiles.

"Look inside," she urges.

Something shiny is puddled at the bottom. I tilt the bag and pour out a gossamer-fine chain, from which dangles a tiny ring. *The* ring.

I catch my breath.

"It was his idea to put it on a chain for you," Charlotte explains softly.

So Charlotte has heard from him. I don't feel jealousy — only the sweetest sense of peace. Again, I realize that there are things I might not yet know about the spirit world. Perhaps, wherever he is, Nathaniel can still commune with someone like Charlotte, who is more experienced than I am. Perhaps I will be able to fully possess my gift someday.

I close my fingers around the necklace, pressing it into my flesh. It radiates warmth, and when I open my hand, the sun glints off the gold and casts a rainbow around the room.

Charlotte whispers, "There wasn't time to get it engraved."

An uneasy thought flickers through my mind: engraved, meaning *in the grave*, and I have been so preoccupied with graves and gravestones, with the dead and undead. She threads the chain through the ring. "It's a gift," she says, carefully fastening the chain behind my neck.

The ring drops with a whisper-soft *pling* to my throat, like a sweet, reassuring touch. I know then I'll always wear the ring, no matter where life may take me. I'll wear it as a memory. A legacy.

I'm too choked up to speak at first, but I manage to thank Charlotte, and give her a hug. She hugs me back, and says, "I'm sorry I wasn't more in touch with you the last week, Lori. I wanted to be sure you figured out things with Nathaniel on your own terms. Do you forgive me?"

"Of course," I tell her, blinking away my tears. I know Charlotte will never be a replacement for Jocelyn, but she's a good friend. A true friend. Like someone else I know.

I wipe my eyes, collecting myself, then go upstairs to call Evan. I think I'll be joining him for dinner tonight after all.